FROM HATE TO DATE

THE WHY CHOOSE CHRONICLES

MIKA LANE

HEADLANDS PUBLISHING

COPYRIGHT

1

LIVVY

"YOU SHOULDN'T BE SO picky, Olive."

My sister still talks to me like I'm the little brat she's been pushing around since we were kids.

Why did I take her call? It's never the best way to start my day.

Actually, her calls are to be avoided any time of the day. I know this.

And yet.

Worse still are the warning bells jabbing at my already-irritated nerves. I spot Mrs. Perkins one block away. Headed right towards me.

I dart across the street, dodging a cab and a confused tourist on a rental bike, causing both to hit their brakes hard. It's worth risking my life though, because Mrs. Perkins thinks nothing of asking me to expel her dog's anal glands every time she sees me.

Because of this, her dog hates me and growls his displeasure whenever I'm around. If it wasn't weird, I'd growl right back at him because I hate him and his anal glands too. I can't blame him, though. I'd hate the person who poked at my backside on a regular basis.

Thank god I don't have anal glands is all I can think every time I work on some dog's.

"Olive? Are you listening?"

Is my sister actually calling me *Olive*? Like she forgot the nickname I've used exclusively since I was in middle school? "Really? Really, Krista? We are having this conversation *again*? And please stop calling me Olive. You're not Mom."

She sighs at full volume, just like my mother does when she's frustrated. Two peas in a pod they are, even wearing matching outfits from time to time. I've tried explaining that twinning with your mom is something most grow out of when they are... I don't know? Twelve years old?

But she's not deterred. I'm surprised she doesn't let Mom crawl right into her marriage bed.

"Okay. *Livvy,*" she draws out, like my nickname feels dirty in her mouth, "it's just that Carter and I were talking and well, you know, you don't have a lot of options. We both agree you should give Deck another chance."

Oh for god's sake. First, what kind of horrible

parents name their kid 'Deck,' and second, is she *still* trying to match me with him?

I draw a slow, steady breath. *I will not fight with her. I will not.* "So you guys think I don't have a lot of options? That's nice, Krista. Nice of Carter too. Didn't know you guys thought I was such a bottom-dweller. Thanks for clueing me in."

I want to be angry, to rage, to tell her that she and her douchebag 'hubby', who make an insufferable couple I call Kritter—Krista plus Carter—can go to hell. But the lump in my throat would give away my hurt and anger, and if there's one thing I don't want to do right now, it's give my perfect sister more power over me.

I lean against an anemic tree, one of several the city of New York planted on my street a couple years ago at the insistence of my local neighborhood group. I'm careful not to put much weight on it because the poor thing hasn't done very well for itself—a light touch causes a cascade of leaves to flutter to the ground. They land on me, getting stuck in my struggle bun topknot, a style my sister never hesitates to tell me is lazy and sloppy.

I will away my tears so I can defend myself, and while I do, I watch Mrs. Perkins, thankfully on the opposite side of the street, meander with her anally-challenged pooch. With her terrible eyesight, she'll never see me, so I really don't need to hide, but I do because that makes me feel like less of a total asshole.

While Krista is extolling—again—the virtues of my brother-in-law's nose-picking buddy, I spot a man hoofing it down the sidewalk at full speed.

This person, I don't need to hide from. He will not ask me about anal glands. But I don't want to meet his gaze, either. So, I hold the phone up to my ear and knit my brow like I'm on a very important call and cannot possibly acknowledge anyone else in the world. Not even if they are bleeding out in front of me, about to meet their maker.

Nope, sorry. Much too busy doing Very Important Things.

I always avoid this man, even though he makes my knees weak with his dark-wash denim jeans, white-soled dress shoes (all the rage among New York's snappy dressers), and fitted vest over a white oxford shirt. I'll never say hello, even though his rolled-up sleeves show off a crazy kaleidoscope of tattoos on some nicely muscular forearms, and his bushy hipster beard is trimmed to perfection.

I won't interact with him, even though I know his name is Owen Whitlocke and he is one of the owners of the trendy and massively successful restaurant East-Side, right next door to my own shop, Pawsh Pets. I call him and his partners the bistro boys. They don't know this, of course.

I also happen to know he's twenty-nine years old, his parents went through a divorce when he was a kid, and he has twinkling hazel eyes, even though I've never actually seen them up close. Arthur, my neighbor and gay BFF shared these gems after dinner at EastSide one night where his sole intention was to determine which team Owen played for.

Newsflash—*not* Arthur's team, much to his disappointment.

But that means he *does* play for my team, Arthur informed me, as if he were giving me Owen as some sort of gift.

Problem is, guys like Owen don't date girls like me.

They don't even know we exist, evidenced by his blowing right past me, arguing on his phone about how many reservations they can fit in tonight.

No, I get to date the guy my sister and brother-in-law think I'm barely worthy of, even if his name is Deck and he picks his nose in public.

I trot after Owen, of course from a distance, once there's no chance of his seeing me. There are just a few city blocks until we reach our respective businesses, so I wrap up my miserable call with Krista. I call it miserable because, thanks to her relentless pressure, I agree to go out with the nose picker *one last time.*

One last time, because, as we know, *I can't afford to be so picky.* That's how much of a bottom-dweller I am.

That's how *my* day is starting.

2

LIVVY

As soon as Owen unlocks the front door to EastSide, I scurry across the street from where I'm hiding or rather, spying on him. Too bad we didn't have a few more blocks to go so I could continue to admire his muscular ass, perfectly encased by a pair of Levi's.

Once he's inside the restaurant and there's no chance of coming face-to-face with him, I push up my own security gate to open my upscale pet boutique.

I love saying that. *My boutique.*

All mine. Mine, mine, mine.

Until I opened Pawsh Pets, I never had much of my own. Not my own bedroom, not my own clothes, not even my own books. The house I grew up in was small enough that Krista and I had to share a room, and because we were basically the same size, we shared clothes too. Which really was the ultimate insult because I was on the losing end of nearly every fight over them.

Thank God, our reading tastes were different, even though everything on our shelves was 'co-owned,' a term my mother liked to use to make sharing sound fun and cool. The books I knew Krista would never open were the ones I wrote my name in, large and possessive on the title page. No one would ever know, because no one but me would ever read these books. At last, I owned something. They might have been mine only because no one else wanted them, but I didn't care. To me, they were still mine.

I worked two, sometimes three jobs at a time for years, saving every last penny to open Pawsh. When it came down to it, no big surprise, I didn't have enough cash. Luckily, because my parents splurged on a fancy-ass wedding for my sister to impress her new in-laws, they took pity on me and gave me what they would have spent on *my* wedding, something that would surely never happen because hey—I'm Livvy, Krista is Krista, and she's the pretty one who gets the guy.

Yeah, their vote of nonconfidence stung, but in the end, I got Pawsh, and that's all that really mattered.

The bells on the front door jingle as I enter, and Harry, the world's laziest cat and Pawsh resident, opens one eye from his perch to see who's disturbing his sleep. When he finds it's me, he turns over with a grunt and gets back to snoozing.

When I opened Pawsh, I thought it would be cool to have a store cat, like a mascot, living here as a permanent fixture, who people in the neighborhood would stop by and say hi to and offer a nice scritch under the chin. Instead, Harry—named after Prince Harry thanks to his ginger color—has turned out to be the most unpleasant pet anyone could ever had. He hisses at our customers, yowls at me for his food, and can't be bothered to move from his perch. I won't complain too much, though. At least he gets up to go potty in his box. It's like he knows I'd draw the line at an incontinent feline and give him the boot from his sweet setup here to a new home, God forbid a family with children who would expect him to interact.

Before I set out my organic dog treats in the front window, chilled overnight to the perfect consistency, I stop for a moment to admire the shop with its bleached pine shelves stocked with all things pet-related, from cashmere cat beds to Swarovski-studded dog leashes. Everything's tidy and in its place. To the quick observer, Pawsh is more a peaceful day spa for humans than a place to get high-end trinkets for fur babies.

But as hip as the place is, it unfortunately doesn't smell like a spa due to the stinky scent of raw, organic pet food, my daily reminder to flick on the expensive air filter one of my dog food reps convinced me to buy.

Baby works like a champ, especially with my cedar-juniper reed diffuser.

While the air filter whirs quietly, I arrange the Jenga-like display of pet treats in my front window, wondering if Owen Whitlocke, of this morning's titillating sighting and the restaurant next door, or his partners, might happen by. While I am under no illusion they'll stop and chat, or even smile and wave, it's always nice to see any of the trio. Seriously. How is it that three perfect specimens of maleness banded together to open one of the hottest restaurants on Manhattan's Upper East Side?

Some people have all the luck. These guys have been blessed with good looks, success, and probably more women than they know what to do with.

Just as I take a photo of the store's front window for the Pawsh Pets Instagram account, which is up to a whopping two hundred followers, most of them the kids who visited the store on a school trip last month, the phone screeches. I run for it, remembering I turned it up to full blast yesterday when I was working in the back.

Harry, who's already hissed at me twice this morning, glares at the disturbance.

"Livvy?" a shaky voice asks when I pick up the receiver.

Oh boy.

"Hi Jewel. What's up?" I ask my shop assistant.

Between the two of us, it's a draw as to who has the

worst love life. Actually, who's to say in the complete absence of a love life like mine, or one that implodes on a monthly basis, like Jewel's?

"Liv, he broke up with me," she says between choking sobs.

I sigh. Jewel has been with me for nearly two years, and the number of calls I've gotten like this are too numerous to count.

"Okay, Jewel, you know what to do. Take some deep breaths, honey."

"Uh… okay."

Her breathing returns to normal for about two seconds, then she gets right back to sobbing.

"Sorry you're upset, Jewel. It sounds terrible," I say, letting her cry it out.

It doesn't matter who she dates. It always ends the same way.

"I… I can't come in t…t…today. I'm s… sorry, Liv," she manages to say.

I shrug even though Harry's the only one who can see me. "It's okay. I don't think we're going to be too busy."

She signs off with a tearful goodbye, and I, satisfied with the way Pawsh Pets looks, grab a seat behind the cash wrap counter and wait for customers and their furry friends to arrive.

3

LIVVY

I DON'T HAVE to wait long before Mrs. Johnson comes in with her overweight beagle. I swear, if I had a dollar for every time the woman asked me for dietary advice for that dog—and never bothered to follow it—I might have another whole steady income stream for the store.

I bend down to scratch the beagle's ears, and when he looks at Harry like he might be a tasty snack, the cat bares his teeth. The message is lost on the beagle, who tries to jump but is too chubby to follow through.

"Now, Mrs. Johnson, what did the vet say when you took this little guy in last week?"

She avoids my gaze, like a bad kid in trouble. "Oh, well, he did say my boy is a little overweight…"

Exactly what I told her the vet would say. One

doesn't have to be an expert to recognize that a dog whose stomach almost drags on the ground is too *well-fed*, as I tactfully put it to her.

I place my hand on Mrs. Johnson's arm to let her know I'm on her side, and nod, looking at the chubby pupper with all the admiration I can muster. "He's such a handsome boy. We want him to be around as long as possible, right?"

Mrs. Johnson's eyes well up. "Yes," she says in a breaking voice. "But I don't know what to do. He's always so… hungry."

I skip the speech about the pet owner being the 'leader of the pack,' and how Mrs. Johnson needs to be the boss and not the other way around. I've tried it a few times over the years, and pet owners don't want to hear it, at least not from me.

So I do the only other thing I can think of.

Sell her some of my very expensive, air-dried, organic lamb dog food.

Hey, a girl's got to make a living, right?

And this stuff is so fancy-schmancy high-end all-natural, it could have its own stand at the freaking farmer's market.

Mrs. Johnson carefully reads the label on the bag of dog food, dreamily running her finger over its promise to 'help unleash your dog's true potential.'

I really wish they didn't market like that. Talk about over promising. I don't know that a chubby, spoiled beagle will ever be making much of a mark on the world.

She leaned close to me even though there was no one around except for our pets, and whispered. "Do you… think it will give him gas? Because he gets awful gas."

After assuring her if there were any issues with the dog food she could return it, I placed a ten-pound bag into her wheeled grocery cart. I made her promise to let me know how the dog liked it, and she was off, smiling broadly and telling her boy he didn't have to go on a diet alone, that she'd join him.

Another satisfied customer.

I am straightening up my inventory of dog leashes, all hanging on the wall in order of size, when another neighborhood local, Tim, strolls in with his parrot on his shoulder.

"Livvy the lovely," he booms.

"Livvy the lovely," the parrot repeats.

"Hi there. And how are you, Polly?" I ask. Who names a parrot *Polly*? So basic.

"How are you, Polly? How are you?" she repeats five more times.

I'm not sure I could handle an obnoxious parrot, although she listens better than some men I've dated.

Polly balks a few times and after turning in circles on Tim's shoulder, settles down facing away from me. It takes me a moment to figure out why she turned her back, but when I see her staring down Harry, it all becomes clear.

Ah yes. I'd keep an eye on Harry too, if I were a bird.

Tim reaches up and strokes Polly's back. "Polly baby, sing your new song for Livvy. Sing your song."

Polly balks again, continuing to watch the cat. "Livvy has nice tits. Livvy has nice tits."

What?

While I'm recalling that parrots only *parrot*—in other words, repeat what they've heard—Tim's face turns bright red and he chokes on something.

Really?

He waves his hand in a *no big deal* fashion and giggles. "Crazy bird. I don't know where she comes up with half the things she says." His laugh is high and squeaky. I bet he wishes the floor would open up and swallow him.

Hell, *I* wish the floor would open up and swallow him, too.

He grabs some of the special birdseed we carry, especially formulated for *talking* parrots, and when I hand him his bag, he slips me a postcard-sized flyer.

"What's this?" I ask, turning it over in my fingers.

It was one of those club invites that people hand out on street corners. The ones I never take.

He bounces in his shoes a little, his embarrassment of a moment before forgotten. "I'm performing at a comedy club, Livvy," he says with pride.

Oh yeah. He told me he was in an improv class.

"You're performing in clubs now? Cool," I say, knowing I'll throw away the card as soon as he leaves.

He takes it back from me and points to a small line of text. "You see, if you use this card, you can get in for ten percent off. Whaddya say we meet there?"

I have so many questions.

"Um… well, I don't really—"

"Look, Livvy, I've been wanting to ask you out for a while. And I thought, well, I thought that with the ten percent off coupon, you wouldn't be able to say no."

Ten percent off of paying my own way on a date to a comedy club I don't want to go to with a man I couldn't be less interested in?

There is so much wrong here.

While I struggle to say something, anything, he takes a step closer, like he's going to share something confidential. Thank God the cash wrap desk is between us. Still, I can smell his coffee breath. It's not pleasant.

"I get in for free since I'm performing," he continues. "I don't get paid, newbies like me never do, so the free entrance is sort of like payment. You know?"

I try to nod and show I understand, but all I do is rock forward from the waist like some sort of stiff-limbed zombie.

"Okay, then," he says, giving Polly a nice stroke down her back.

Harry's in his predator crouch, so I put my hand on him, pretending to stroke his fur, but really restraining him in case he gets an idea about pouncing. I've never seen him go after any animal in the store, not yet, anyway. I thought he was too cool to do that, but now I'm realizing he can't be trusted. He is a killer, and that's not good.

"See ya, Livvy," Tim says, heading for the door. Before he's gone, he turns back. "Say thank you, Polly. Thank Livvy for the yummy birdseed."

She glances sideways at me as she rocks from one leg to the other on his shoulder, then squawks and lets loose again. "Livvy has nice tits. Livvy has—"

The front door jingles as Tim runs.

I look down at the card he left me, with its promise of a rocking good time and ten percent off the twenty-dollar admission. A two-dollar savings. Wow.

Jesus.

Is this as good as it gets? Are my romantic choices limited to cheapskate Tim and his dirty-mouthed bird, or a dork named Deck, who picks his nose in public?

Is this all you're going to give me, Universe?

4

LIVVY

I NEVER EXPECTED Pawsh Pets to be a goldmine. Sure, Swarovski-studded dog collars and cashmere cat beds fetch a pretty penny, but you can only sell so many. The pet food flies out the door, but it's got a much lower margin to compete with Pet Outlet and huge stores like that. Which is fine. All I ever wanted was to earn enough to cover the store's rent, keep the merchandise fresh, and pay myself a livable wage for getting by in New York City. I don't think that's too much to ask. I've never had dreams of owning a weekend getaway like so many New Yorkers, and travel isn't really my thing. Hell, I'm pretty much tied to the store anyway, especially with a flaky assistant like Jewel. She's great and all. She works hard when she's here.

The key is, *when she's here.*

I know I provide an important service to the neighborhood. I even got written up in the paper last year as one of the top ten pet stores in the city. Of course, I had to contact a hundred of my customers to vote for me, but it was really fun to see Pawsh Pets in the paper. It boosted business, and I was super busy for a while.

Some might think, like my sister and brother-in-law, the Kritters, that the things I sell are silly and frivolous. Maybe they are, but I also help find homes for a lot of dogs and cats from the local animal shelter. Of course, the Kritters get pets only from breeders, so they don't even consider my volunteerism important, hard as that is to believe.

And now, as the end of the business day approaches, I stop rearranging merchandise and take a seat at my desk to get ready for the only part of the job I don't like —facing the bills.

It isn't cheap to run a business in New York, and over the last couple weeks I've seen more money going out the door than coming in. I'm not panicking—I'm sure it's just the time of year or something. The big-box pet store across town could never take away any of my business.

Actually, I'm not sure about that. Not sure at all.

I kick my shoes off in my little office, which is really just a storage closet stacked high with inventory, and stare down at what feels like a mountain of invoices. And late notices.

Yes, late notices.

Maybe I can just drop them all into my desk drawer and pretend they don't exist.

Great idea, Livvy.

With more bills to pay than cash in my checking account, I do exactly that, at least for the time being. I will take care of them, just not today. For now, they're *poof*, gone.

I wander to the front of the store to peek out front and make sure there's no dog poop on the sidewalk. People seem to think that I don't mind picking up their dog's mess because, why else would I be in this business? A couple times a day, I have to go out and clean the mess people leave behind.

For me.

I could pretend not to notice, but the number of people who've yelled at me after stepping in it forced me to act.

As if I, personally, crapped on the sidewalk.

The coast is clear, as it has been all day, leaving me wondering if I might see any of the hotties from next door wander by, when I realize the smells wafting my way indicate they are probably neck deep in preparing for the evening's customers.

There is one thing that catches my eye, though, and it's a new 'for sale' sign in the window of the business across the street.

What the hell?

The business, a women's shoes store, was there yesterday.

But it's not there anymore, as if it disappeared overnight.

Actually, it *did* disappear overnight.

I'd been in the shop a couple times to check things out. Never bought anything as I mostly live in Birkenstocks and sneakers, but they had nice stuff. And now the place is empty and dark. Someone even spray painted the name off the awning.

I'd heard of businesses in the city that clear out their inventory and disappear in the middle of the night to avoid paying bills.

A scratchy uncertainty washes over me, and I shiver even though the shop is more warm than cool with the sun shining in. Then, I see someone come out of the store and lock the front door behind himself.

The landlord. I know him. He has three dogs.

He sees me looking out the window and waves, then hustles across the street to me while dodging traffic.

"Hi there," I say, opening the door for him.

"Livvy, hi." He purses his lips. He's clearly upset.

"What's going on over there? What happened to the shoe store?" I ask.

He rolls his shoulders and cracks his neck, a sure sign he's having a shitty day. "The fuckers split overnight. Owed me six months back rent. They took every last shoe and piece of furniture that wasn't nailed down."

"Oh my God. I'm so sorry."

"Did you see anything? Did they tell you anything?" he asks.

I shake my head. "They never really talked to me when they realized I wasn't going to buy any shoes," I say with a weak laugh. "I'm really sorry."

He shakes his head. "Oh well. Guess it's a write off. Let me get some dog food while I'm here."

I hand him a basket and he starts filling it.

Wow. A business splitting in the middle of the night.

"You sure you didn't see anything, Livvy?" he asks again.

"I'm sorry, but I'm usually out of here before dark. I was probably gone well before they did the deed."

But I do know who might know something—the guys in the restaurant next door. Does that mean I now have an excuse to talk to them?

Thank you, Universe.

5

OWEN

WHEN THE LAST customer from lunch filters out and the prep cooks are getting things ready for dinner, I finally take a deep breath. Weston's up in the office crunching numbers or something, and Enzo's in the kitchen scolding someone for dropping a very expensive cut of meat on the floor. I know this because I can hear him yelling over the blaring house music we allow in the 'quiet hours,' the short time we're closed between lunch and dinner.

Funny thing is, these quiet hours are anything but, with employees joking around, just-washed pots and pans clanging together, and the local farming co-op bringing in last-minute items for the night's service. We're fully booked and it's going to be a wild one.

I love it. I really do. I love every positive thing about the business, from our top selling dishes and most expensive bottle of wine, to the negative things liked clogged grease traps and no-show employees. Nothing can kill the feeling I have when I'm at EastSide.

I type tonight's dinner menu into my laptop so I can send it to the printer down the street. Normally, we have crap like this done a day or two in advance, but we never got our sunchokes today and they were supposed to be served with our smoked-seared squab.

It's a bummer, but shit like this happens all the time in the restaurant business. You just have to roll with it.

I click *send*, and look at my watch. I have a special arrangement with the counter girl at the print shop, who works on my stuff as soon as she gets it. It's our secret, of course—we can't let the other local businesses know I'm jumping the queue. In return, I bring my friend there a tasty treat.

"Dude," I call to one of the kitchen guys, "can you package me up something for the girl at the printer? Maybe one of those pine Pavlovas?"

He hustles off to the cooler while I check my phone. I'm not a big fan of the pine-infused Pavlova, but Enzo insisted on it, saying 'resin flavors are the next big thing.' I'm not sure I agree, but the man's got good instincts. I save my battles for other things.

Heading down to the printer, boxed dessert in hand, I notice the shop across the street is dark, with a *for rent* sign in the window. Wasn't that place open for business just yesterday? I can't be sure. Because it was a women's shoe store, I never paid much attention. Aside from the beautiful women working there.

I zip past Pawsh Pets, where a pissed-off looking cat is sitting in the front window batting a beat-up toy. I've shopped there a few times and the owner—whose name I can never remember—is always helpful. A bit of an odd young woman smelling of citrus and wearing socks with her Birkenstocks, but beautiful in a girl-next-door sort of way. Not at all glamorous like so many other women in New York City, and especially not like those who frequent my restaurant. There was something comfortable about her as she pulled a pen out of the mass of hair gathered on top of her head, and hand-wrote my receipt. I almost told her about my cat Cheddar, but no one knows I have a pet feline. I just said I was picking up something for my mother's cat.

Today she must be in the back of the shop. The cat stares me down as I pass by, showing its teeth once or twice.

I deliver the Pavlova to my inside girl, who runs to bring me my menus the moment I walk in. A couple other patrons look our way when I hand over her treats, and she blushes as she coos, "Thank you, Owen."

She's a sweet thing. But just a kid.

On my way back to EastSide, I duck into the corner market.

"I don't know why you drink that shit," Sal says

when I plop two sixes of Bud Lite on the counter in front of him.

The man loves to bust my balls.

We've had this conversation a hundred times. "I told you, Sal, I get tired of that fancy Japanese stuff we have over at the restaurant. Sometimes a guy just wants his Bud."

He snorts. "Owen, even I don't drink that stuff."

I raise my hands in surrender. "Look, you can be as prissy as you want about your beer. It's all good, my man."

Sal scowls. Actually, he always scowls. He'd look put out if he won the damn lottery. It's like his face is fixed that way. I do get a smile out of him from time to time, but even then, it's only half a smile. "Yeah, yeah. What-ever you say, pretty boy," he snickers, handing me my package.

But I don't leave just yet. I want something else. I'm just not sure what.

I look around the market, pretty much like every other one in the city, with its small, overpriced, but convenient selection of necessities—some canned goods, some questionable produce, and lots of junk food and alcoholic beverages. Then I spot what I want.

Sal snorts his disapproval again. "Goddamn, Owe, don't tell me you eat this crap. With all the fancy shit you got over there, like sea urchin balls and such, you want chips and onion dip?" He wrinkles his nose in outright disgust.

Which makes me laugh.

He adds the new items to my bag, shaking his head like my lowbrow purchases are a personal insult. "Don't you get decent food at the restaurant? For *free*?"

I shrug one shoulder. The paradox of restaurant life. "Look, just because someone works in a restaurant doesn't mean they get to eat there. It's busy during mealtimes and besides, sometimes I want a goddamn potato chip. Ya know? Sea urchin balls don't always cut it. But I appreciate your looking out for me, Sal. You'll make somebody a nice wife someday."

He scoffs and waves me out of the store. "Yeah, yeah. Get out of here, pretty boy. And trim that damn beard."

I wave goodbye over my shoulder.

Love that guy.

6

OWEN

Eight quick hours later, the customers are gone and Weston, Enzo, and I are ourselves. I grab the Bud Lite from the back of the walk-in cooler, where I hid it in a box marked *lard* to keep sticky fingers off it, and break open a cold one at our favorite table, a corner banquette where we can see the whole restaurant.

I raise a bottle and the guys join me. "To another killer dinner service, gentlemen. Boys, we are officially minted motherfuckers. How many restaurants are profitable in their first two years?"

"I dunno, but we are, motherfuckers!" Enzo hollers, still in his food-stained chef jacket.

"That's right," Weston adds. "You know you've

arrived when people are more interested in Instagramming their food than eating it."

Another record-breaking month. It doesn't get any better. Except for a great review from the local paper, which put us on the map in only month two.

Thank you, restaurant critics.

"I don't even care that two teenagers were caught having sex in the ladies' room tonight. Let them have at it. Nothing's going to ruin this," I laugh.

I couldn't get mad, anyway. I did the same thing back in the day. Only I wasn't stupid enough to get caught.

Enzo slams his fist on the table, rattling the beer cans. "Guys, we are the Kardashians of the culinary world. Well, with less drama and more talent."

Weston's head snaps in his direction. "What? What the fuck are you talking about?"

Enzo holds his hands up. "Whoa, brother. Calm down."

Weston leans away from Enzo like he's got something contagious. "Dude, we are nothing like the Kardashians. And anyway, you don't watch them, do you?"

Enzo looks at me for backup. But he has to get himself out of this one.

"I, well, um, no. But my nonna does, and sometimes when I'm visiting, she'll have it on in the background. She loves those girls."

We're silent for a moment as Weston and I look at

each other. Then, in a burst of laughter, he slaps his thigh. "Dude! You watch the Kardashians. I knew it!"

We continue giving Enzo shit until he's well and truly sorry he ever mentioned anything about them or his beloved grandma.

I crack open another Bud and lean back in the booth to look around.

Fuck me.

I never thought I'd have a restaurant, never mind one as successful as EastSide. Doing what I love with a great team? It doesn't get any better.

What a long way I've come.

I got into cooking out of necessity. After my parents' divorce, my mother had to go back to work, leaving me on my own. If I wanted to eat, I had to make something.

It was that simple.

Picture me, a twelve-year-old boy, home alone at dinner time, scouring the internet for something easy to make for dinner because I was tired of cereal and milk. I graduated to hotdogs, then spaghetti, and not long after that, I was on my way. I'd take frozen food out of the freezer before I left for school in the morning so it would be thawed in time for my return. By the time I was thirteen, I could roast a chicken. Of course, I destroyed the kitchen in the process, something my mother was not happy about.

I made the mistake of telling the kids at school about my cooking acumen, only to end up being called *housewife*. That got me into a few fights. I learned how to cook and fight at the same time. I still cook but haven't kicked anyone's ass in a while.

The food I make these days is, of course, more sophisticated, but every now and then I roast a chicken the same simple way I did when I was a kid. It's just as delicious.

I've never told the guys any of this. It's stupid, I know. Self-sufficiency for a kid is good, but those weren't my happiest days. When I think back, it's sad I was home alone, fending for myself. My friends' mothers were putting on great spreads for the whole family to enjoy around the dinner table. Everyone else had a mom to feed them, but for me, it was the other way around.

7

OWEN

NEXT MORNING, the day's deliveries arrive, and instead of standing there like a useless asshole, I help the driver, a pimply kid from the Bronx, unload the truck. I need the exercise, anyway.

Meanwhile, Weston stands there in his starched khakis and button-down shirt, his hair slicked back like a preppy Ralph Lauren model, checking off the delivery against our order.

He looks over the crates of meat, fish, and vegetables. "Where's the cultured butter?"

The kid stops in the middle of passing me a box and gives Weston a blank look. "Uh, what?"

Yeah, I'm sure this kid knows what cultured butter

is. Hell, I only recently heard of it for the first time and I'm in the damn business.

I give Weston a look to let it go. "We'll get Enzo to make some for us. We have plenty of time."

I pile the boxes and crates onto a hand truck as the kid drives away, but before I go back inside with Weston, I spot our neighbor, from the pet store, breaking down some boxes in the alley. There's no way she doesn't know we're right here, and yet she doesn't look over or acknowledge us. It's a shame. She's a good-looking girl. Guess we guys are not her type.

Weston follows me to the kitchen. I pass everything off to one of the staff, wipe my hands on a towel, and check my jeans and shirt to make sure they're still relatively clean. I hate getting dirty before the day's even started.

"Hey, do you have a minute?" Weston asks, tapping on his iPad where he stores every last detail of the business.

I nod, and he waves over Enzo, who doesn't look happy at the extra task he now has, of making the special butter. I get it. The man's got a shitload of things to do. But it's these little details that make East-Side what it is. Sure, we could use regular butter and maybe our guests wouldn't know, but *we* would. We're not in this to be *regular*. Even though it means we're committed to a fuckload of work.

"What's up, Wes?" he asks, wiping his hands on his

chef's jacket. He goes through several a day. I know, because Weston complains about the laundry bill.

As the numbers guy, I suppose that's his job.

"So, guys, a couple of our investors are interested in helping us expand," he says.

Holy shit.

This is Weston's dream come true. He loves the business side of things, and intuitively understands how it all fits together. His analytical abilities blow my mind.

Enzo's eyes widen, a huge grin taking over his face.

My reaction is different. I say nothing. My face remains neutral. After all, this could be very good. Or very bad.

"*Fuck yeah,*" Enzo hollers, pumping his fist into the air, then high-fiving with Weston.

I'm silent until they turn to me. I'm not surprised by Weston's news, nor pleased or displeased. More like skeptical. The success of EastSide always seemed inevitable to Weston and Enzo. I see things differently than they do, being the pessimist of the three of us. "That's cool. Let's hear more."

Weston starts going over numbers, talking about things like average sales per table, median length of stay at peak hour, and dine-in versus carry-out profits, but when Enzo and he start going back and forth on reasonable recipe yields, my eyes glaze over.

My role in EastSide, at least on the day-to-day, is to manage 'front of house' operations. I greet the guests, manage the servers, hosts, and bartenders, and handle any customer issues. I don't deal with the numbers like Weston does. He loves that shit. I like knowing what the numbers tell us, the story of whether or not we're making money and how much, but I don't like the process of working with them. No thanks.

I snap out of my reverie when someone mentions Pawsh Pets.

"Wait, what? What about Pawsh Pets?" I ask.

Weston slaps me on the shoulder. "Owe, man, listen up, okay? Enz and I were just brainstorming. If we *do* decide to expand, how do we do it? It's not like there's an empty building next door, just waiting for us."

One of many challenges, I am glad he realizes. That's my pessimist coming out.

"Yeah, no shit, Wes. There's an apartment building on one side of us, and that weird pet store on the other," Enzo adds.

I scoffed. "What's weird about it?"

He has no idea I've shopped there.

Enzo shrugs. "I dunno. Have you seen the people who go in there? Total eccentrics. And I hear they have dog beds and shit that cost five hundred dollars."

"Do I need to remind you we have bottles of wine that cost three times that much?" I ask.

He hangs his head and laughs. "You got me there, brother."

Weston lowers his voice when he realizes we've

gotten the attention of the entire kitchen crew. "Guys, look. I don't think the woman over there is doing such a bang-up business. Sure, people go in and out of the place, but with the rents we pay here, you'd have to sell a hell of a lot of dog food to pay the bills. I mean, like truckloads. Unless she's independently wealthy and has money to burn, I imagine the going is rough for her."

Enzo presses his lips together and nods. "True. And what about that shoe store across the street that disappeared overnight? What's up with that? They're there one moment, gone the next. Are we the only business on the block that's killing it? Beside Sal's corner market?"

Weston exhales a big sigh. "She might be ready to throw in the towel with a little prodding and the right offer. It seems quiet over there, at least to me. And, yeah, she's... different. I imagine she's the kind of woman who spends her free time wasting away in bed reading romance novels. I mean, when we see her in the alley, she pretends we're not there. Anyway, here's what I'm thinking... what do you say to us putting together a friendly proposal for buying out her lease? The worst that can happen is that she says no. She already can't stand us, apparently, so it's not like we're losing anything on that front."

Holy shit. Not that I'm friends with the woman or anything, but I feel for her. It's callous, how the guys are talking about her business.

"Have you two forgotten what it's like to pour your heart and soul into something? Christ, have some compassion for the woman," I say.

Enzo narrows his eyes. "Dude. You're sweet on her. Aren't you?"

I scoff as indignantly as I can. "Enz, I don't even know her name. And when was the last time you saw me going out with a woman who wears socks and Birkenstocks?"

The guys laugh and nod, and I feel like shit for mocking the woman with them. The few times I've spoken with her, she seemed nice enough, if a bit shy. She doesn't deserve to be laughed at by us assholes.

"You know what else bugs me about that place next door?" Enzo asks, now clearly fired up. He wants Pawsh Pets *gone*. "There's dog shit out in front of the place all the time. Fucking nasty."

"No, there isn't."

"I stepped in it just last week."

"Dude, that was one time. She cleans it up, I've seen her. She's good about it. If you're dealing with pets, you're also dealing with their poop."

Enzo shakes his head, curly hair flying around his face. "Well, one time was enough for me. I can't work in the kitchen with dog shit on my shoes."

He has a point. "Okay, okay, I get it. But Enz, you can step in dog shit anywhere in the city. People are slobs, not picking that stuff up. At least the girl cleans up after her lazy customers."

Weston and Enzo stare at me.

I don't blame them. Why am I defending someone I don't even know?

8

OWEN

As lunch service ends and we gear up for dinner, I have a few moments to think over Weston's expansion proposal. Am I down with it? I keep going back and forth. We're already working so hard, I want to make sure we still have some fun. And in the best of circumstances, restaurants are risky businesses.

Enzo jumped on board without a second thought, but I'm not like him. I'm not like either of those guys. Weston has money to fall back on, thanks to his loaded father, and Enzo has a huge family that adores him and has his back.

Me, I have only my mother. She's been trying to make ends meet since I was eight years old, when my father left for work one day and never returned. I help her out, but she still toils as a teacher's assistant, taking summer jobs for extra cash. We've had a lot of challenges, the two of us, so I don't have the rosy outlook on life the other guys do. I can't just assume things will work out, because I know they sometimes don't. That's what happens to a kid whose dad is coaching little league one day, and then forgets about him the next. You're waiting for the other shoe to drop any time something good happens. Like you don't deserve it.

So, I have my shit story, although it's not any shittier than anyone else's. We all have our demons to face down.

But if today's lunch service showed me anything, it's that Weston is without a doubt on the right track. We could for sure benefit from expanding our space— we turned away almost as many parties as we sat, the kind of problem every restaurant would kill to have. Think of all the money we might have made if we'd accommodated those people.

"Yo," Weston says, coming downstairs from his tiny, cramped office. "Today's lunch crowd looked good."

I nod. "It was good. Really good. We would do well to make the place bigger, Wes."

Yeah, Weston's sold me on the idea, although I'm still on the fence about asking the woman next door for her store space. I know I wouldn't like it if someone did that to me. It just feels like a dick move.

Weston sinks into the banquette seat next to me.

"We'll make the woman next door an offer. It'll be interesting to see how she reacts."

"What do you mean?"

"The one time I talked to her, I saw her out front when I was coming in. I stopped to chat, and she took the opportunity to tell me she could smell the meat we were cooking. I told her I hope she liked it, and she announced she was a vegetarian. And then, I'm pretty sure she sneered at me," Weston says.

I wave away his concerns. "Whatever, lots of people are vegetarian these days. Besides, we always have at least one veg option on the menu."

"Yeah. I told her that. Afterwards, I invited her to the quarterly investor party to, you know, make nice. You should have heard her excuse for not coming."

"Really?"

He grimaces. "She said she'd be expressing some dog's anal glands that night."

"*What?*"

"I know, right? She actually told me that. Hell if I didn't feel like the biggest chump in the world," he adds, obviously still stinging from the rejection.

I started to shake, and then I couldn't hide that I was laughing my ass off. "Dude, that is so classic. Talk about the biggest blow-off in the history of blow-offs."

I couldn't stop laughing.

The woman was a baller, first letting Weston know she could smell our 'meat,' and then turning down a dinner invite in order to do something to a poor dog's anal whatever.

Fucking hilarious.

But the bottom line is, at least at this point in time, she does not seem to be one of our biggest fans. In fact, *she* would probably like to see *us* go away.

"So..." I start to say once I've caught my breath, "sounds like we need to proceed carefully."

"Absolutely. But everyone has a price. At least, that's what my father says." He looks out the front door of the restaurant, momentarily lost in thought.

Yeah. Weston and his father. Talk about a fraught relationship. I used to think money solved everything, but the opposite is actually true.

"She is pretty..." I say without thinking.

Weston's gaze snaps in my direction. "*Ha*. You do like her."

I shrug one shoulder. "I don't even know her. I only said she's pretty."

"She's got to be something of a decent business-woman, operating a shop in New York City. But with the right offer, she'll consider it. She'd be crazy not to." He points a finger at me. "You, Owen, will take the lead."

"What? No way. You know I hate numbers."

Weston rolls his eyes. "I'll prep you. Don't worry about that."

"But you're the business guy. Shouldn't the pitch come from you?" I ask.

"Normally, yes. But this is different. You're the charmer. You know how to make people feel good."

I shake my head. "I don't know, man. What if she starts talking about cat litter or something like that?"

Or dog's anal stuff?

He pats my shoulder. "This is where your skill comes in, my friend. You have an uncanny talent for working with people. If she's going to listen to any of us, it will be you."

I roll my eyes. Talk about being persuasive. Weston uses flattery like our kitchen uses butter. "Yeah, right, I'll seduce her with spreadsheets."

He laughs. "Hey, some women like numbers. And you think she's pretty. She'll pick up on that. It'll make her feel good. Special. Women like to feel special. Hell, invite her over here for a drink. She can try out that new, unfiltered, organic rosé we just got. Vegetarians love organic shit, right?"

"What if she says she has to clean some poor dog's... you know?" I ask.

"You tell her yours need cleaning too."

9

LIVVY

"OH, SETTLE DOWN, HARRY." I rub the cat's head. He gives me the stink eye, which is pretty much his permanent expression, anyway.

And for the second time, he hisses at Arthur, the neighborhood gadabout and my gay BFF, who hisses right back at him.

"Don't do that, Arthur. It'll just upset him more. Cats are delicate creatures."

Arthur huffs. "*I'm* a delicate creature. And since I'm higher on the food chain than that orange terror, I expect him to bow down to me and not the other way around."

Time to change the subject and fast. "Hey, I like

those huaraches. Are those the ones you got on your boys' trip to Ibiza last year?"

Distracted by my compliment, the frown on his face dissolves and he looks down at his shoes in memory of an amazing, debauched vacation. But it doesn't last long. "Hey. You're trying to redirect. Don't forget, I know you, Livvy."

When he takes a seat, I know he's sticking around for a while. I set aside the cat food inventory I'm working on and slide my exacto knife along the taped edge of the box the UPS guy just dropped off.

Who Arthur and I nearly drooled over. How is it that UPS hires such good-looking men? Or should I say *people*? The female who came by a couple months ago was adorable. I bet every guy in town wants to carry her packages.

I pull out a spaghetti tangle of dog leashes. I don't know why the distributor can't pack them more nicely. People hardly ever make the effort to do things right. I don't understand. It's not that hard to take pride in your work.

Things like that really bug me.

Arthur continues griping about my cat. "I don't know why you keep that nasty animal. He hates everybody."

"No, he doesn't hate everybody. He just hates you."

Arthur scoffs with world-class indignation.

The door jingles and we look up to see the mailman drop off what looks like bills.

Lovely.

"Afternoon, everyone," he calls before he leaves.

"Afternoon," Arthur sings after him.

I stop organizing leashes. "Is he, you know, on your team? That mailman?"

Arthur rolls his eyes. "It doesn't matter. He may or may not be. I can still admire him, you know. Nothing wrong with that." He picks up my mail and starts nosing through it, shaking an envelope and holding it up to the light.

I'd normally be annoyed by that, someone looking at my mail. But Arthur is… Arthur.

"Things seem a little quiet around here," he says.

What does he want? A marching band?

"No. It's just early in the day. That's all."

He sniffs like I'm bullshitting him, and I guess I am. Who the hell am I kidding? I've been open three hours and not a single customer has stopped in.

A nervousness, a sense of unease, one I've been repressing for weeks, makes its way to the surface. It's as if Arthur's observation, his saying out loud what I've been trying to pretend isn't happening, opened some sort of gate. It doesn't feel good. And I know it's time to be honest with myself.

But not just yet.

"It will be fine," I insist. "Not every day has people streaming in and out. It's the nature of retail. It was the same way with the shoe store across the street. Well, the one that used to be across the street."

He cranes his neck to see out the window and clucks his tongue at the sight of the deserted boutique.

People around here do not like a blight on their neighborhood. I'm surprised a petition hasn't already gone around, demanding that *some*one do *some*thing.

Like it's that easy.

"Yeah, well, you see what happened to them. And the Pet Outlet across town seems to be doing a lot of business."

I swing my gaze in his direction. "What are you saying, Arthur? That Pawsh Pets is going under? Thanks. I'd think you could be a little more support-ive," I snap.

His eyes widen at my tone.

No one understands how important this place is to me. It's my home. It's part of me. What would I be if I didn't have it?

I finish tagging the new dog leashes and start hanging them on the wall. Arthur glares out the front window, my mail still in his hand, to avoid looking at me. I get it. We're annoyed with each other. But we'll forget it ever happened in a minute or two.

Or sooner.

"Wow. This looks like quite the invite you've received, Livvy," he says, holding a cream envelope.

"An invite? To what?" I wipe my hands on my work smock and take it from him. It's made of thick paper and is heavy. Like a high-end wedding invitation.

How do I know this? My sister's wedding, of course.

"Livvy, looks like you got an engraved invitation from the three culinary musketeers next door."

What guys next door?

Oh. Shit.

EastSide invited me to something?

Why?

Is one of the guys getting married and he's just inviting the whole damn neighborhood?

Ugh. I hate weddings. Well, I didn't before my sister's. But I do now.

I shudder when I think of the poorly fitting pink dress in the back of my closet. And the stupid, drunk groomsmen, especially the one who grabbed my ass. The worst was that half the guests got sick from bad shrimp. And my sister still considers it the best day of her life.

My aversion to weddings aside, I turn the invitation over and over, relishing the smooth, creamy paper and its perfect, sharp corners. Its weightiness in my hand somehow encompasses all that is right and perfect. They even spelled my name right, as much as I hate it. Olive Fontaine.

So many people think it's Olivia, but no, it's just good old Olive.

For a moment I am honored, which is stupid, because I don't even know what's inside the envelope. Hell, they could be recruiting me as a dishwashing intern, for all I know. But hey, whatever they're having over there might put me in touch with a deep-pocketed crowd of pet owners.

Here comes Pawsh Pets' brand ambassador, people.

Arthur drums his fingers, bursting my bubble. "Well. I didn't get one," he sniffs.

"How do you know? Maybe it's sitting in your mailbox."

He harrumphs. "First, I get my mail in the morning, and the only thing I got today was a catalog for Harry and David's. Second, I'd never get an invite anyway, thanks to that queen of a head waiter I slept with last year. Some people are so vindictive."

I carefully lift the envelope flap and remove a simple card inviting me to the restaurant tomorrow night.

Tomorrow night!

Arthur snatches the card from me. "Ugh. How pretentious. The recommended dress is 'elegant.'" He gags, like Harry does when he has a hairball.

"Why don't you come with me? I'll sneak you in. You can be my plus-one. What do I care? I don't have anyone to impress."

If they never invite me back, so be it.

Arthur lifts his chin. I'm pretty sure I insulted him, something that's very easy to do. "I do *not* have to sneak into parties, I'll have you know. Over my dead body would I go there, with or without you."

I shrug. "Suit yourself."

He gives me an up and down look, overflowing with disapproval. "You can't go looking like that."

Really?

He looks at his watch. "What time are you done here? We need to get you ready. Do you have anything nice to wear?"

"Um, well, I have a nice wrap dress—"

He shuts me up with a wave. "That'll do. It'll have to.

10

LIVVY

NOT TWENTY-FOUR HOURS LATER, I am sucking my stomach in like Arthur told me to, after he scolded me for not having any Spanx on hand. I also have my shoulders pulled back, although not as far as I was instructed to because no human can walk that way. The challenge is that the wrap dress is low cut, so Arthur told me not to wear a bra. But if I move the wrong way, everyone and their mother will see my boobs.

How he knows so much about women's undergarments, I do not want to know.

I'm doing okay in the Jimmy Choo stilettos I saved from my sister's wedding, but I'm watching for any sort of crack or bump on the sidewalk that could send me tumbling. I thought about wearing sneakers or even my Birks, and then putting the heels on when I arrived, but Arthur wouldn't hear of it.

So, I'm mincing down the street, thanking God I only have to walk a few blocks.

I hear and smell the party before I get there, the tinkling jazz seeping out onto the sidewalk, not to mention the smell of more meat than I'd like to think about.

Walking through the door is like arriving on the set of the TV show Bachelor, with all the beautiful people, beautifully dressed, sipping beautiful cocktails, and having beautiful conversations. I nearly wince from the perfection of it, but remember the posture lessons Arthur gave me, and to purse my lips slightly to elevate my cheek bones. I'm wearing Stepford Wife-level pleasantness, not at all my usual style, but if it helps me blend in and make connections that can help Pawsh, then a little facial cramping is well worth it.

I just hope they have a carrot stick or two for me to nibble on.

A hand lands on my elbow and I turn to see Owen, whom I've met once in the shop.

"Oh, hi," I say, sticking my hand out straight for a shake.

"Olive—" he starts to say.

"Hey, who told you that's my name?"

Jesus, girl, calm down.

"Oh, well, you're in the neighborhood registry. You know, the one that lists all the shops and such?"

Goddamn, he's good-looking, and even in my heels, I still look up at him.

"Yeah. That's right. That's how I know your name is Owen Whitlocke. Well, please call me Livvy. I hate Olive. It was my grandmother's name, and she was an awful, awful person. She sent my dad off to an orphanage when he was only—"

"Livvy, I want you to formally meet my business partners." His smile never wavers as he masterfully cuts me off with more charm than is humanly possible.

He waves over the other two guys I've passed on the street a couple times and spotted from our shared alley, who are equally, freakishly, good-looking. And friendly. And happy to see me.

A wave of... I don't know... maybe discomfort? passes over me. These three masters of the universe, eager to meet me with their outstretched hands and perfect teeth, remind me of the alarm I felt when the popular girls in high school were nice to me. Turned out they wanted to copy my homework.

This time around, I have no homework to offer these guys. Do I have something else they want? Are they after free dog food? Kitty litter?

I'm waiting for the other shoe to drop, but they're so damn nice, chatting me up like they really give a shit about me, which I know they don't, but the attention is nice all the same, if only for a few minutes.

I'm sure they'll be on to some other guest momentarily, leaving me sipping my cranberry cocktail in the corner through one of those minuscule straws that are really meant for stirring.

These men, Owen, Weston, and Enzo, were crafted by gods, and in particular, the god of haute cuisine, should one exist.

If the curly-haired one, Enzo, isn't already perfect enough, he points out his nonna across the room, wearing a somber black dress, her silver hair piled on her head, but smiling at the constant flow of people fawning over her.

He's either a genuinely nice guy laying it on thick for the 'awe' factor, or he's a genuine mama's boy. Or rather, grandmama's boy.

I cut to the chase, through the bullshit, with the foremost thing on my mind. I don't want to waste anyone's time, and I don't want mine wasted either.

"Hey, look, guys," I say in a quiet voice.

They take a step closer to hear me and they smell really, really good.

"I might as well just tell you now, I can't afford to eat here. You don't have to be all nice to me and stuff."

I look from one to the other, proud of myself for letting them off the hook.

They stare back.

Then Owen laughs awkwardly, followed by Weston, and Enzo points toward his nonna.

"Gotta go check on my grandmother." He bolts.

"I do appreciate your inviting me, though," I say so they don't think I'm an ingrate. "Which way is the ladies' room, please?"

As polite as ever, Weston steers me in the direction, and I stroll through the crowd, stomach in and chest out. As soon as I'm alone, I sit on the edge of the toilet seat and relax, my stomach pooching like a normal woman's, and my dress falling open, because who's going to see my boobs in here?

I look around at the wood-paneled stall and marvel over its real door, not one of those janky metal things with gaps so big you have no privacy, and I hear someone else enter the ladies' room.

"Jesus, he can't keep his eyes off her. I don't want to make a scene, but I will if I have to."

Oooh. Drama. I press my ear against the door. The voice is familiar.

"Honey, take my word, men are always looking. Don't let it be personal. Just because your husband is staring at that woman from the pet store, it doesn't mean a thing. And don't worry, she's nothing special."

What? *I'm* the woman from the pet store!

They're talking about *me*.

But *who's* looking at me? And who's talking about me?

And I'm *nothing special*? What a bitch.

"I know she's a beautiful young woman, and that Diane von Furstenberg dress fits like it was made for her but..."

They think my dress is a *Diane von Furstenberg*? I snort, and when the conversation halts, I quickly flush the toilet to cover my noise. Footsteps hustle for the ladies' room door, which immediately opens and closes. I peek out and when I'm sure I'm alone, exit. I take a look at myself in the mirror, turn sideways, then do my best to get a view of my butt.

Huh. I mean, I guess I look nice. But in this party full of New York glamazons? No way. I adopt Arthur's posture again, lift my chin just because, and return to the party.

I hear the voice again.

I inch toward it, pretending to be reaching for a glass of champagne, when a quick glance tells me it's the city councilperson's wife. Bartlett Murray's wife is trash-talking me?

Bartlett Murray was staring at *me*?

These are some strange people.

Not yet defeated, I strut through the party as Arthur instructed me to, weaving among the dark suit jackets and glittery dresses worn by the sort of people who spend a hundred dollars on a scented candle for their guest bath room.

I find something that looks like a carrot stick, but because I am not positive it is, I don't risk eating it.

I pull a fistful of mini-postcards out of my pocket, a combination calling card and buy-one-get-one coupon, and drop a few on the tray of a passing cocktail waitress. She smiles kindly and slips one into her pocket. I am encouraged. I cruise over to a table covered with tiny goodie bags—I guess party favors?—and place cards into several.

Who knew EastSide would turn out to be such a useful marketing platform?

I drop cards onto other tables where people are coming and going, and when I look up, I realize my efforts have been under the watchful eye of the trio of handsomeness.

So much for my covert ops. Or should I say, covert *oops*?

As they make their way toward me, it's clear my business acumen isn't earning me any brownie points. But I don't care. My mother always says it's the irritation that makes the pearl. If I can't be an influencer, being irritating is the next best thing.

I look around, wondering if I could make a clean escape. I should thank the guys, but I'm not feeling even that gracious.

Let them be stars in their own Michelin-rated show. I am and always will be a taco truck girl.

As long as it's vegetarian.

11

WESTON

LIVVY LEFT the party like her pants were on fire. We tried to say goodbye but she was too fast for us.

We had plans to charm and woo her, but to be honest, when it came down to it, I wasn't looking forward to it. Not at all. It's not in my nature to be disingenuous. I grew up surrounded by fake-ass bullshit like that and swore I'd never be that way.

And yet here I am. Just another asshole trying to make a buck by stepping on someone else's back.

When the investors first approached me, and I shared their expansion idea with the guys, it sounded so easy. Get the woman next door to sell us her lease, get her the hell out, and double our space. Easy, right?

But when she came to our party, the fact that there's

a living, breathing human being on the other side of our shared wall, who probably has the same hopes and dreams I do, smacked me right in the face.

And by the way, she sure cleans up nice.

The few times I've seen her in passing or through the window of her boutique, she's always a bit of a mess. A cute mess, but a mess nevertheless, with her hair piled on top of her head, sensible shoes, and a smock, I guess designed to keep enthusiastic pets from jumping on her clothes. Because I'm usually in a rush, or thinking about the restaurant, I never give her any more thought than that.

Big mistake.

When she arrived at our party last night, I nearly choked on my bourbon.

I instantly knew who she was—she wasn't that unrecognizable—but her slinky dress, sky-high heels, and sleek hairstyle threw me for a loop. I didn't see that coming.

But what I found perhaps most charming was her nervous babble. She wasn't at all studied in the art of conversation like most women I meet, who carefully measure every word, so aware they are of how they're perceived. When she told us she couldn't afford to eat in EastSide, I was amused but my heart also broke a little at the same time, slapping me in the face with a reminder of my privilege.

She had a point. Lots of people cannot afford to eat

in a place like EastSide. And I want to do something about that.

When I found her looking over the untouched buffet table—people rarely eat at fancy functions like this—she pointed out a couple things.

"That's veal tongue carpaccio."

She looked like she might vomit.

"Would you like to try some snail caviar?" I asked, reaching for a cracker.

She stared me down. "I am a vegetarian. Do you have any fresh veggies? Maybe with dip?"

I looked over the table like we might actually have something like that, but I was really just stalling for time.

I kept to myself that this is not the kind of place that serves a crudité platter, and that we provide a different perspective on food. That's not the kind of thing she wanted to hear and, besides, I try not to insult people.

Instead, I pointed out our 'Walk in the Forest' mushroom dish, garnished with hazelnuts and chickpeas.

She looked at me like I was speaking a foreign language, so before she could say anything else, I scooped some onto a spoon and aimed it right for her mouth. I came at her so fast, she automatically opened, like little baby being fed.

She wrapped her perfect bow-shaped lips around

my spoon and when the taste hit her, closed her eyes and moaned a little.

Fucking awesome.

"That... that was incredible," she said, swallowing the bite I gave her.

It was incredible for me too, but for different reasons. Just ask the stirring below my belt.

Another unexpected treat of the evening.

I excused myself to go greet our city councilperson, so left her to decide whether she wanted more 'Walk in the Forest.'

I lost track of her after that. After all, we'd invited nearly sixty people, but when Enzo pointed out her guerrilla marketing efforts—scattering around her Pawsh Pets announcements—well, I almost want to run over and help her. But duty called and we guys, amused as hell, let her do her thing.

I liked that about her. But I also like the space her business occupies and haven't changed my mind about acquiring it. Just how we might approach her.

At midnight, when everyone but the cleaning crew is gone, Owen pulls his beloved Bud Lite out of its hiding place and we sit for a minute.

"Another great party," he said, raising his bottle.

I hate Bud Lite but can tolerate one for my friend.

Enzo leans onto the table and lowers his voice. "What about Olive-known-as-Livvy? Think we made any inroads?"

His choice of words makes me cringe. But business is business.

"Well, she left when she realized we saw her giving out her business cards. That was a ballsy move, but I have to give her credit for it. Maybe she'll get some new customers," Owen says.

"Well, we'll go over and talk to her, maybe tomorrow. Our numbers are good, and we can make her a solid offer. Clearly, she needs to be handled with kid gloves, but our payout is more than she'd net in five years. She could take the money and open a shop in a small town where rent is cheaper and there's no big box competition," I say.

"Do you think she'll consider the offer?" Enzo asks. "Or will she lose her shit and throw us out? That's how someone in my family would do it. Just saying."

I laugh. "Really? Has your nonna ever kicked you out of her house?"

Enzo's eyebrows rise. "Are you kidding? Dude, she might be eighty years old with a cane, but she can still beat my ass if she wants."

"What do you do when she comes after you?" Owen asks, laughing.

"I *run*. Do you think I'm an idiot? You don't mess with women in the Messina family."

"Well, I don't think Livvy is the type to come after us with a weapon, but she's prickly and clearly doesn't suffer fools. If she doesn't like what we bring her, I have no doubt her words will be delivered with just as much painful intent," I say.

Owen nods. "Yeah. She may be resistant. But everyone has their price, right?"

12

WESTON

WE SAUNTER into Pawsh Pets with a proposal that could turn Livvy into the kind of businesswoman she's only ever dreamed of being, thanks to our investors and, of course, my own personal money. When my grandfather died, he left my siblings and me a nice chunk of change that not even my bastard father could touch. And believe me, he wanted to get his hands on it. But a good trustee managed it until I reached twenty-five. I'd like to think I'm using the money wisely now that I have full access to it, and that my grandfather would approve.

I know others who don't.

While I don't see much of my father, he doesn't hold back when it comes to sharing his opinions about my involvement in EastSide. In fact, he never hesitates to announce how most restaurants fail in their first year and that only a lucky twenty percent ever make a profit.

Well, we're two years into it and are already profitable, which is why both our investors and I feel comfortable with expanding our operations.

"Have either of you guys ever been in there, in Pawsh Pets?" I ask as we head next door.

Enzo shakes his head, but Owen clears his throat and coughs a little. "Yeah. I've been in there. Picking up some stuff for… my mother."

"Your mother eats cat food?" Enzo laughs.

"Har-har, funny guy."

"Enzo, you go in first. You're the one who brought your nonna. Brownie points, you know," Owen says.

He frowns. "What? That woman can't stand me. She can't stand any of us. She hates everything we represent. I could smell the disdain dripping off her last night."

Ouch.

Not sure I agree, but still, best to proceed with caution.

The bells hanging on the door blast our arrival, and a young woman with spiky purple hair and several facial piercings looks up, her face covered in surprise.

I guess she's not used to three men coming in together, with no pets.

"May I help you?" she asks in an authoritative voice.

I step up. "I'm Wes, and these are my business partners, Owen and Enzo. We're from EastSide, just next door."

She considers us. "I know EastSide is next door. Livvy told me she went to a party there last night."

I bet that's not all she told her.

"And what's your name?" Enzo asks.

Brave man.

"Jewel."

"Well, Jewel, we're here to see Livvy," I say, looking around and hoping she appears quickly. Talking to this Gen Z kid is not my idea of fun.

She rolls her shoulders as if our request is a burden. "She's at the gyno," she says, snapping her gum.

What? Did she say *gyno*?

"Oh, um, did you say *gyno*?" Weston asks with all the politeness he can muster.

Ugh. I can't believe he repeated it.

Jewel nods. "Yeah. She has some kind of infection or something, I think."

Oh my god, this kid needs a muzzle.

"Okay, well, we're sorry to hear that. Do you know when she's due back?" I ask.

She looks at the cat clock on the wall and screws up her face. "Not really. Guess it depends on how bad the infection is."

Enzo is green around the gills and starts moving toward the door like he might catch something. "Alrighty then, we'll just come back."

But as he reaches for the door, Livvy appears on the other side of it. He opens it for her, the damn bell drowning out every other sound on the block.

"Hello. This is a surprise," she says, her face a question mark.

She's back to looking like her normal self, 'cocktail party Livvy' having been put away. And now that I'm taking the time to check her out, everyday Livvy is actually pretty cute, in an unmade-bed sort of way.

"Um, sorry, Livvy," Enzo says, taking a couple steps back from her. "Jewel told us about your health problem."

She frowns. "What health problem? Jewel, what did you tell these guys?"

"I told them you were at the gyno with some sort of infection."

Livvy's face turns several shades of pink before it settles on magenta. Goddamn, she is cute.

"I was at the bank making a deposit. Why did you think I was at the… doctor, Jewel?" she asks.

"Oh, I didn't." She turns to us guys. "It's just that I'm in acting classes. Our last assignment was to make someone feel real uncomfortable. How do you think I did?" she asks, beaming.

Livvy points to the back of the store. "Hey, can you go through the boxes that just came in, Jewel?"

She looks disappointed she can't practice on us anymore and gets up in a huff. It's beyond me how this woman even has a job.

Livvy turns back to us, still blushing. I don't blame her. "Sorry about that. She's kind of a… free spirit."

"No worries," I say, stealing a glance at Owen to start his pitch. "Hey, I hope you enjoyed yourself last night."

She stiffens, maybe bracing herself for a scolding.

But that's not why we're here.

"Wes tells me you liked the 'Walk in the Forest' mushrooms," Owen says, smiling brightly.

Maybe too brightly. Dude needs to tone it down. The woman is not an idiot. She's going to suspect something. Which she would be right to.

"They were really good," she says carefully.

After an awkward moment, I jump back in. "Livvy, do you have a moment? There's something important we want to discuss with you."

"What's that?" she asks, alarmed.

She looks from one of us to the other, already on the defensive.

This is so not going to work. We should have just sent our lawyers. Which would be shitty, of course, even more shitty than what we're doing right now.

But hey, it's just business.

I finger the folder in my hand that contains all the numbers I've crunched as well as the initial offer for the purchase. Of course, I expect her to counter our proposal.

I cut to the chase. "We'd like to buy you out of this space so we can expand EastSide."

Color drains from her face, and her mouth drops open.

Uh-oh.

But because I have her attention, I continue with my pitch, which sounds more and more pitiful with every word.

That's when the doorbell screeches again. An elderly woman with a dog breezes in. Or should I say a *dog* with an *elderly* person walks in? The dog is definitely the one in control.

"Hello, hello, hello," she calls, waving at all of us. "Busy here today, huh?"

She brushes past Enzo, where the top of her head just reaches his elbow, and lets the dog leash go, like the shop is a safe place for him.

But that doesn't mean *we* are safe from him.

"Oh, Mrs. Perkins," Livvy starts to say, "can you keep ahold of Sinbad? You know how... enthusiastic he gets."

Put out, Mrs. Perkins sighs and turns just in time for her charge to lift a hind leg and relieve himself. Right on one of Owen's expensive Italian shoes.

Owen jumps, but it's too late. His shoe, sock, and the leg of his pants are wet with dog pee.

Mrs. Perkins reaches for Sinbad's leash, but he runs away. When I try to help, he snatches the business proposal out of my hand, runs to a corner, and sinks his teeth into my handiwork, chomping hungrily.

Owen shakes his leg like that will get rid of the dog

pee, I dodge Sinbad's sharp canines to get my mangled papers back, and Enzo dives for his leash, knocking over a tower of pet aromatherapy ampules.

Mrs. Perkins adds to the commotion by alternately screaming at the dog and then at us, accusing us of poisoning him with our papers. Livvy's eyes are wide with abject shock, horror, and helplessness.

You can't make this shit up.

13

WESTON

"Stop! Everybody stop!" Livvy shrieks, waving her arms like some kind of movie director hollering *cut* in the middle of a botched scene.

Her outburst is so bloodcurdling, everyone stops for a moment, even the damn dog. "Gentlemen, *out*," she yells, pointing at the door.

No problem, lady, like we really want to be here, for fuck's sake. I can't speak for the guys, but I'm out of this freakshow. The general humiliation and irritation at the thwarting of my five-star pitch has me realizing I should have just stayed in bed all day and watched porn.

Just as Owen, Enzo, and I inch towards the door, like we're afraid to turn our backs on the madness,

Mrs. Perkins calmly picks up Sinbad's leash. The dog drops the papers he's already destroyed, and, with great authority, Mrs. Perkins inexplicably passes the leash to Enzo.

"Please take him out back, honey, for a poo-poo. It's his time," she says sweetly.

"Oh my god," Livvy whispers.

Enzo, bless him, shrugs and takes the leash.

"Mrs. Perkins, these men do not work for me—" Livvy starts to say.

But Enzo raises his hand to stop her. "It's okay. I don't mind." He heads for the back of the shop to find his way out, Sinbad and poop bags in tow.

Mrs. Perkins returns to fingering the Swarovski-studded dog collars as if she's choosing a color, humming an old, vaguely familiar show tune.

"Hey, don't forget to pick it up, young man. You know dog shit is all over this city," she calls after Enzo.

My god. What have I just witnessed?

"I'm so sorry," Livvy whispers to Owen and me. "She has really poor eyesight."

I catch Owen biting his lip, his face turning red. He starts to shake and I realize he's trying his damnedest not to laugh. Of course, this kicks off my own case of uncontrolled chuckling, and I race for the door with Owen on my heels. Once outside, we let it rip.

Finally back in the clean, pet-free safety of my office in EastSide, Owen smells like urine, my proposal looks like it was attacked by Jaws, and when Enzo returns, he's traumatized by the sheer volume of Sinbad's feces. We sit quietly, trying to understand the chaos of the last fifteen minutes.

Is that placed cursed or something? I've never seen anything go from okay to shit quite that fast.

After his adrenaline stops racing, Enzo gets to his feet. "Well, guys, I gotta get to work." He quietly leaves, shaking his head. Owen is right behind him.

Before we left, I put a bottle of champagne on ice for a celebration. No need for that now.

I close the door to the office and put my head in my hands. As I replay all that went down, and how I might have improved, my cell rings.

It's my mother. Shit, I hope no one died.

That's pretty much the only time she calls.

"Mother. What's wrong?"

Her laugh tinkles over the phone line, which really means nothing. Mother always laughs like that, no matter what is going on.

You could tell her she won the lottery, or that the world is coming to an end, and she'd still giggle lightly. I've never been sure whether it comes from nervousness or plain old indifference. But it's her calling card.

It's strangely comforting to hear her voice after Livvy's unequivocal smack-down. I feel like a little boy who was just pushed off the playground swings, running to his mother for comfort.

Get it together, asshole.

"Weston, hello, darling. It's been ages."

"I know, Mother. Is something wrong? Is Dad okay?"

"Everything's fine, fine, fine. I heard you had a little gathering the other night at the restaurant. Sounds like it was quite the soirée."

Goddamn. She has spies everywhere.

"We did, Mother. It was a great success."

I don't ask her how she found out. It doesn't matter, and besides, it's not like it was some kind of big secret.

"Yes, that's what I heard. The food and drinks were flowing for all your friends. How lovely you can do that for the people you care about."

Oh.

Okay.

I get it now.

"What are you getting at, Mother?"

I know what she's getting at. I just want to make her say it. This is our thing. We test each other. I've talked to many a therapist about breaking out of this mold. Nothing ever works. I fall into the same damn pattern every damn time.

"What do you *think* I'm getting at, Weston?"

And so, we continue with our dance, going 'round and 'round to see who blinks first. It's usually me, just like it is this time.

"You're upset you weren't invited, is that it?"

She sniffs. "Oh, I don't know that I'm upset. But an invitation would have been nice."

"But you know you'd never come. Dad wants

nothing to do with EastSide. Besides, this was for investors only."

Well, also people next door to us with space we might want to expand into.

"Oh, honey. Why don't you let us invest?"

She elevates crazy-making to a professional level.

"Mother, you and Dad didn't want to invest. You were adamantly opposed to my entering the restaurant business, remember? Said it was silly, a losing proposition, for dreamers. That restaurants never make money, and that my imminent failure would bring embarrassment to the family."

I don't have to think hard to remember their objections to EastSide, because when they hurled them my way, the harshness of their words seared my psyche like an ugly tattoo. I'd like to forget it. Be the bigger person. Move on. All that shit. Not sure it will ever happen.

And what was left unsaid, but understood by everyone, was not so much that a failed restaurant on my part would embarrass the family. No, the embarrassment part stemmed from my refusal to seize a predestined role in the family business. Dad's vanity is such that any independent decision made is a rejection of him and everything about him.

Why would I want anyone like that at my party?

14

LIVVY

"Jewel, what's this sticky stuff?"

I high-step out of whatever's on the floor of Pawsh Pets, readjusting the house slippers I forgot the change out of before I left my apartment.

Jewel opened the shop for me today, leaving me a little extra time in the morning to feel sorry for myself and the insult I am still stinging from at the hands of the bistro boys from EastSide.

Even if they did take Mrs. Perkins' dog out to go potty.

The nerve of those jerks. To waltz right in—during business hours! When I have customers!—and ask me to bail on my much-loved boutique so they can have more tables to push more of their carnivorous delicacies.

They can go right to hell.

I'm not going anywhere.

"Oh hey, Livvy. How are you this morning?" Jewel asks, running up from the back of the shop, all casual and stuff even though she's supposed to be hanging out in the front of the store, where we greet our customers.

"The floor's sticky, Jewel. What happened here?"

She nods enthusiastically. "Oh my God. It was the greatest thing. You see, I spilled my smoothie. Fucking thing went splat, all over. But Harry"—she turns to point to the orange devil himself—"slurped up the entire thing."

She puts her hands on her hips and shakes her head like she can barely believe her good fortune.

Um, not so fast.

I take a look at Harry, blissfully snoozing on a full stomach of too much dairy and too much sugar, and wonder when it's going to come back up. Because it always does.

I want to kill her.

"Jewel. Adult cats are not supposed to have dairy, and certainly not sugar."

She scratches her head. "But Livvy, it was a win-win. Harry got a treat, and I didn't have to clean up," she says cheerfully.

Good God.

I go back to my storage closet-as-an-office before I say something I'll regret. I'm already in enough of a tizzy, remembering I have a date tonight with my brother-in-law's creepy coworker, the nose picker. What the hell was I thinking when I said yes?

Actually, I know what I was thinking. Get my sister off my back. Saying yes was my only option. And now I'm dreading it so badly my stomach is in knots. I've got to get out of it.

But how?

I spy the exacto knife we use for opening shipments. I could sever a finger. Or wander into the street and get hit by a cab.

Either of those would work well.

But something less bloody would be even better.

Then, the bells on the front door announce a visitor. Maybe this will take my mind off my anxiety.

If only.

"Well, hello, Bartlett. Nice to see you," I say, extending my hand to our skinny, balding, local councilperson. The same one whose wife trash-talked me.

"How's your little puppy?" I ask, forcing a smile.

His eyes dart around the shop, avoiding my gaze. I glance at Jewel behind him, and she raises one eyebrow.

"Well, um, we had to um, get rid of him," he mumbles in a quiet voice.

"*WHAT?*"

Shit. I didn't mean to holler.

My outburst grabs his attention, and his gaze finally meets mine. "She was, well, she was peeing all over the house. We brought her back to the breeder."

Holy crap. I know some pet owners are more savvy than others, but this is the work of a total idiot. I am about to tell him that dogs' bathroom habits need to be trained. But Jewel knows what I want to say and shakes her head *no* in warning. She's right to remind me to keep my mouth shut.

"Yeah. It wasn't what the missus and I wanted. But… you know. We'll get another dog at some point. Hopefully one smart enough not to pee all over."

What an ass.

He claps his hands, signaling an end to the dog conversation, and I wonder why he's here. It's surely not to stock up on dog food.

"Saw you at the EastSide gathering the other night," he says. "Didn't get to say hi. Sorry 'bout that."

"Well, your wife did. Sort of." I laugh.

I really need to just shut up right now. But that's not going to happen.

"She did?"

I nod. "Yup. Overheard her talking about me in the ladies' room. Something about someone staring at me, even though I'm nothing special."

His eyes bulge while his complexion goes through a contortion of unhealthy-looking colors, starting with bright red, and I get the feeling he'd rather die than be here right now.

Chalk one up for *me*.

"I overheard them from the stall I was in," I add, relishing in the torture.

Ugh. I need to stop.

His mouth opens and then closes, and then he does what any politician does best—he changes the subject.

"You know, Livvy, I wanted to stop by today and just catch up." He wanders through the shop, picking up things from the shelves and putting them back. "Hey, how is this organic catnip doing?"

He turns the flowery box over, which looks more like a package holding expensive soap, to read the tiny print. Which I know he can't. I have excellent vision, and not even I can read those damn things.

"The catnip has sold okay. Honestly, Bartlett, things have been a little slow."

His head snaps in my direction. "Really?"

I shrug. "Yeah. All businesses have ups and downs. What can you do besides wait it out?"

His gaze drills me. "Pack it in," he says quietly.

"Excuse me? What's that?" I ask.

Holy shit. Did the bistro boys send him over? Tell him to help get rid of me?

I'll kill him. Then, I'll kill the guys. After that, I'll open a vegetarian restaurant in their place and donate a portion of the proceeds to the Humane Society.

Those fuckers will learn what I'm made of.

"Wh… why would you suggest that, Bartlett? You know how business works. Everyone has ups and downs. Why would you think I'd throw in the towel so easily?"

His eyes dart around as he backpedals. "Oh. I didn't mean that. I mean, if you think you can make it, then go for it, for heaven's sake. But look, I recently got some information you might be interested in."

"Yeah? What's that?" I ask, watching perspiration droplets run down his temple.

How did someone like this even get elected?

"I got word at a recent council meeting, Livvy, that a big shot developer's looking to buy up the block."

My stomach drops to the bottom of my sticky Birkenstocks, and I want to hurl.

"Wh… what do you mean? What does that mean, exactly?" I stammer, certain I misheard him.

Right?

Jewel is at my side in an instant and puts a hand on my arm. For as clueless as she is, she's still a good friend.

Bartlett picks up steam when he sees my wilting. "Yeah. It's kind of exciting. They want to put up condos on the entire block. Build a little park. That sort of thing. Could be a done deal, from what I know," he says cheerfully.

"What about the businesses on the block, like mine, and EastSide next door?"

"Oh my," he says, looking at his watch, "I'm late for a meeting. Let's put a pin in this and circle back later."

He and his clichéd work-speak disappear out the door.

I stumble over to the cash wrap and take the seat Jewel was occupying. "Oh my God. What does this mean? Holy shit." I drop my head into my hands.

Jewel comes over to rub my back. "That's crazy, Livvy. Geez."

Holy shit. Two vultures looking to displace me. As if business wasn't already hard enough. It's just me against them and all their money and connections and futuristic thinking.

Why did I even get out of bed this morning?

Jewel reaches for her backpack and starts rummaging around. "Here," she says, extending an open palm to me. "Have an edible. It'll make you relax, forget your problems for a while."

I look down at the tin she twists the cap off of, and inside are pretty little candies coated in sugar. I reach for one but stop.

I do not need to be high right now. Or ever.

"No. I don't want that, Jewel. Why did you even bring them here?"

She turns her nose up at my squareness. "Fine. Calm down. It's legal here in New York, in case you forgot."

She picks up one of the candies and pops in into her

mouth. "Suit yourself," she says, putting her edibles back in her pack.

I'm speechless.

"You know, Livvy, I can always ask my dad for money to help you. He likes businesses that I support."

"Thanks but I don't need edibles, and I don't need your father's money."

I'll figure this shit out on my own before I become a footnote in some tycoon's greedy legacy.

15

LIVVY

I PACE AROUND PAWSH PETS, thinking about the bistro boys' proposal, and now the developer's plans.

It this meant to be? Is the universe giving me a short window to run my beloved store, and then telling me to get the hell out?

Should I get out?

"I'm heading for lunch," Jewel says, her eyes glazed and half closed.

"It's only ten-thirty," I say.

She smiles and floats out the door. And as she does, Tim comes in with his parrot on his shoulder.

"Livvy, long time no see," he says, trying to close in for a hug.

But I turn to straighten up a shelf, blocking his unwanted advance.

Score one for me.

"Hey, Tim," I call over my shoulder.

"So, didn't see you at my comedy club debut. You gotta stop by. My teacher says I'm as good as Jerry Seinfeld."

This is one of those days where I can't stand people and wonder why I just didn't become a forest ranger living in a lookout tower where I never have to deal with other human beings.

I'm not kidding. After a battery of aptitude tests when I was in high school, that is actually what my guidance counselor told me I should go into.

She might have been right. Except that I hate the outdoors and could never climb a lookout tower due to my fear of heights.

"Oh, Tim, I've been pretty busy."

The parrot on his shoulder shifts from foot to foot when it spots Harry.

"It's okay, Polly," Tim says, stroking her head. "You're safe here in Livvy's shop."

The bird decides to join the conversation. "Livvy. Livvy has great tits. Livvy has great tits," she squawks.

Oh my God. Not that again.

"I really gotta get back to work, Tim."

He grimaces. "Okay. I'll stop by another day when you're not so busy."

As if I don't have enough on my mind.

I finally have the shop to myself for a few minutes, thank God, because my head is absolutely spinning. I don't need one of Jewel's damn edibles. The universe is doing a number on me just fine, all by itself.

The way I see it, I have a few options.

To start with, I can tell the bistro boys to hit the road. Which I already sort of have.

Or, I can tell them that I am, indeed, having some cash flow issues, and that I'd like to know what they are offering. I can just see them circling like vultures, their faces smug and tones patronizing. It's all so humiliating.

Oh. Sorry it didn't work out. Best of luck.

Hey, maybe we can hold a vegetarian going away for you. It's the least we can do.

Or we could name a cocktail after you. Something with no meat, of course.

Ugh.

It's like my pride has an expiration date on it that's coming up really fast.

I reach for the ringing phone when I see it's my sister. Maybe she can distract me from my downward spiral of doom.

"Livvy," she says cheerfully, "are you all ready?" she asks, drawing out the last word.

Shit. Shit, shit, shit.

"Oh my God, Krista, I'm having a crisis."

"What? What happened? Are you okay?" she asks.

I spill the story of my shitty day, and when I'm done, she sighs.

"Krista, you have to get me out of this date. I am so not up for talking to another human being tonight. I don't care what you have to tell him. Say I had a stroke. That I'm on life support. I was bitten by a rabid dog."

"Rabies is pretty much eradicated in house pets, Livvy," she says.

Ugh. Not the point.

"I am in no condition to spend time with another human, and in particular the nose picker."

"Stop calling him that. He's a nice guy. And like Carter says, you should be happy someone is willing to take you out."

"Ha!" I boomed, "so Carter's the one who's saying this. Nice. What a great guy. And to think he's my brother-in-law. How lucky am I? Woo-hoo!" I scream.

I have a mind to tell the Kritters where they can shove their crummy fix-up attempts, but I have more important things on my mind.

"Take care of it, Krista. I am not going."

I end the call with a swipe to my screen.

The conversation with Krista only serves to up my anxiety levels, and now I'm sorry I answered the phone.

First the bistro boys want my shop. Then, some big-ass developer does too. How do I hold my own against these people? I only have myself and a little money in the bank. I don't have investors or deep pockets, or any of that shit.

How will I stand up to these forces? I feel like a soldier with no army.

Then it occurs to me—have the bistro boys been informed about the developer? Would they have come calling like they did, if they had that information? Wouldn't that be bigger fish for them to fry?

I may just have information they don't.

Maybe we can help each other. As much as they are dicks, we do now have a common enemy.

If the developer wins, we're all toast, their stupid expansion plans notwithstanding.

Jewel returns from a very long lunch, and I take the opportunity to run next door.

I'll start by apologizing for handing out business cards at their party.

16

ENZO

"IF THIS IS TRUE, why didn't Bart say something at our party the other night?

Weston sits there, typing numbers into his iPad because adding and subtracting are clearly his happy place, and Owen stares into space, or rather at the tiny water stain on the ceiling from the last rain. These old buildings are charming, but there's no end to the things that go wrong with them.

None of us really knows what to do after the bomb Livvy just laid on us, that some developer is frothing at the mouth over our little block. Except maybe cry. As a behind-the-scenes kitchen guy, I'm not the expert businessperson. Weston is. I don't know what it really means when a huge corporation comes after you.

But I am pretty damn sure it's not a good thing. Nor a slam-dunk, in spite of the fact that our investors are some of the best-connected people in the business. Just like how in the wild, the biggest creature wins, in the down-and-dirty world of business, the biggest pile of cash wins. Sure, EastSide is doing well, especially for a new-ish restaurant, but we're definitely the David to any developer's Goliath.

I'm not a worrier. I believe things work themselves out, maybe not always the way you want them to, but they do work out. So, I naturally gravitate toward the idea that the developer will just wake up one morning and decide he doesn't want our choice little Upper East Side block, and that somewhere else in the city will be far more lucrative—and easier to acquire.

Yes, I've been called naïve before. Overly optimistic. Head-in-the-clouds. A dreamer.

Whatever.

Which is part of the reason the guys and I are such a good team. Our commitment to the restaurant business aside, we balance each other—I'm the positive one, Weston and his love for numbers make him the logical, levelheaded one, and Owen's the we'll-never-make-it realist.

On our own, each of us wouldn't amount to a hill of beans. I learned that early on. But together, we're formidable. If I do say so myself.

"There's got to be some way for us to come out on

top of this. I just need to think," Weston says, rubbing his chin.

Owen rolls his eyes. "Dude, get your head out of the numbers. What if Livvy is trying to screw with us? Sure, we can confirm everything with Bart, but I find it very strange he didn't say a word to us at the party. And what does she mean about *partnering* with us?"

Always the naysayer.

"She probably doesn't have any specific ideas, just like we don't. She's absorbing it all, like we are. Give her the benefit of the doubt, Owe," I say.

Owen's shoes might have been peed on, Weston's papers might have been mangled, and I might have picked up the world's biggest pile of dog crap, but the whole freak show next door was still funny as hell. I like that Livvy. And I full-on respect her first inclination when we told her we wanted her store, to get pissed and kick us the hell out.

I wouldn't have respected her if she had folded at the first negotiation. Hell, if you don't believe in what you're doing, you have no right to be running a business. Passion and dedication are the number one currency, cheesy as that sounds.

If I weren't a thousand percent behind EastSide, as well as in love with kitchen work, there's no way I'd survive the long hours and other hassles the job entails. I'd have bailed long ago.

"What I want to know," Owen says, drumming his fingers on the table, "is how Bart knew about this before we got word. Shouldn't the landlord have reached out, let us know he was entertaining other options? Something is up here."

"I have a call in to the landlord right now," Weston says. "But it doesn't really matter how the information made its way to us. The important thing is that we put together a plan. And I think partnering with Pawsh Pets could be a very good move."

Owen dabs at a drop of coffee spilled on his shirt-sleeve. He's surprisingly anal for someone in the food business. By the end of the day, I'm covered in every-thing I've cooked.

"Wes, you just want to partner with her because you like her. I saw you feeding her our mushroom dish at the party," Owen says.

Weston throws him a sharp look. "Maybe I do. What's not to like? She's different from your typical New York City woman—"

"It didn't hurt that she wasn't wearing a bra that night…" Owen adds.

"Whatever, man. You can't tell me that partnering with a small, woman-owned business won't be the perfect balance to a restaurant like ours. The possibili-ties are endless. Think of the goodwill she brings to the table."

We look at him, waiting.

"Okay. I get it. What good does it do her to partner with us?" Owen asks.

"Our money. Our connections. Don't be such a dolt, Owe," Weston says

Damn.

He continues. "We need a multi-part approach that includes things like community support, help from local authorities, and probably even a lawyer."

Owen rubs his hand over his face. "Fine. That's all fine. But it sounds expensive as hell. We're profitable, but barely. We've earmarked any extra money for growth, and now we have to spend it to save our asses?" He slams a fist on the table, shaking everything.

I ignore his outburst and turn to Weston. "Do you have anything specific in mind, Wes?"

"As a matter of fact, I do, as long as Owen can keep his temper tantrums under control."

I try not to laugh. Their bickering is legendary.

He continues. "What I'm thinking, if Livvy's on board, is some sort of party, kind of like the one we had last week, but a little less fancy. More down-home."

I glance at Owen and see he's listening.

"We can rely on Livvy's customer list and hold a gathering for pet owners, where they actually bring their animals. We'll engage people, get some good PR, and let everyone know we're serious about standing our ground."

Damn. I could seriously get behind that.

"I like it," Owen says slowly. "Throw in free cocktails and dog treats and we've got our own peaceful little protest. We'll invite the city council, of course, and maybe even the landlord. Yeah, man, I can see this working." He gets to his feet. "I think I'll head over to talk to Livvy right now."

He *does* like her. He can't hide shit.

I stand too. "It's time for me to get back in the kitchen for lunch service. You go forth and conquer, Owen. Make us proud," I say smacking him on the back.

I suspect, in addition to pitching her on Weston's event idea, he's also working in a little flirt time with our pretty neighbor. Thank goodness she came to us with the news, and willingness to work with us. She could have left us in the dark, I suppose, but then she'd be hurting herself just as much as us.

The woman is no dummy.

Weston heads to his office to kick off his master plan, and I go to the kitchen to get my hands dirty.

Best part of the day.

17

ENZO

On the night of Wine & Whiskers, so named by Livvy, EastSide is buzzing like a live wire. Dressed-up pet owners are streaming in with dogs in bowties and even a few cats wearing tiaras. You can see it in the guests' faces, how psyched they are to have a party where their pets are welcome, and why not? Who doesn't want to have their best friend by their side? The goodwill in the air as people meet each other's four-legged friends is unmistakable. Talk about the absolute perfect ice breaker. Even the shyest, most awkward person in the world would be able to make small talk at a party like this.

Actually, we have a feathered guest too, a parrot named Polly sitting on the shoulder of a quirky guy named Tim. I swear the bird was squawking about tits, but I can't be sure, and don't really want to find out.

Livvy cruises the party, about a thousand times more confident than she was at the gathering we hosted a couple weeks back. Tonight, this woman is in her element. Nearly everyone knows her. And they clearly adore her. She glides through the crowd in the same sexy dress she wore last time—so she only has one nice dress, who cares?—greeting not only the humans but also their animals. Who knows how all this will play out in the end, whether we'll win or the developers, but it's a nice change here in EastSide to see these folks alongside the well-heeled foodie crowd.

I even got our pastry chef to dig up a recipe for dog treats, and by the way they're being scarfed down by our guest canines, he'll have a new career if he ever tires of preparing people food.

"What do you think?" I ask Livvy when she slows down enough for me to catch up to her.

She's breathless and her cheeks are the sexiest pink. "Thank you so much. Thank you for hosting this. I think we really got the attention of our customers. I have Jewel handing out the flyers telling people who to write to, and a couple have even said they'll help with legal stuff."

Damn.

"Oh look," she says, "there's Bartlett Murray and his wife."

The crowd parts for them, that's how well-known

they are. Or self-promoting. It's hard to tell with them, the neighborhood 'power couple.' Bartlett smiles and shakes hands, giving a thumbs up to the people in the back he can't reach.

Livvy starts to head in the opposite direction, but I catch her arm. "Where are you going? Don't you want to say hi?"

She shakes her head hard. "His wife doesn't like me and I don't want to risk any support we might get from him. You go chat him up."

"She doesn't like you?" I repeat.

But Livvy brings a finger to her lips and gestures with her chin that Bartlett's getting close.

Game on.

"Hey, Enzo," he says, slapping me on the back a little harder than necessary, "you bring that grandmother of yours tonight?"

Nonna can be pretty memorable. If she decides you're worth talking to.

"Not tonight, Bart. She's out playing Bingo."

He guffaws. "Better keep an eye on that old girl, she looks like a heartbreaker."

"Oh, yeah. For sure," I say.

His wife hugs his arm closer, like she doesn't want him to get away, and looks around, if I'm not mistaken, with a certain amount of disdain.

That's funny. She liked EastSide just fine last time she was here.

I wave over a server with a tray of champagne, and hand a glass to each of the Murrays.

"There sure are a lot of… animals in here," she says, looking down like one might be nipping at her ankles. Or peeing on her shoe.

"Don't worry Mrs. Murray, they're all on leashes and are very well behaved. Livvy was careful with the invite list." I lean closer to them and lower my voice. "We couldn't have guests who don't know how to behave, if you know what I mean."

Mrs. Murray grimaces at the thought, and I try not to laugh.

"So, where is our lovely pet shop girl?" Bartlett asks, laughing again.

His wife throws him the stink eye, and I get a sense of what Livvy was referring to.

"She's mingling, Bart. I'm sure she'll be right over to say hi," I lie. "But in the meantime, I wanted to talk to you about the developer looking at our property. I'm curious to know how you found out before we did? Even before our landlord did?"

"You know, Enzo, us folks on the city council are privy to all sorts of information. If someone wants to make a change in the neighborhood, we're the first ones they come to!" he says with pride.

Not sure I buy that.

"Interesting. It seems like the businesses impacted would be the first to know."

Is that even true? Who knows. I'm just fishing to see

what else he knows, and with the ego he has, he'll spill it all just so he can brag.

"Well, Enzo," he says, releasing his wife and swinging an arm around my shoulder, "sometimes the little guy is the last to know." He leans his head down the way you might talk to a kid who just struck out in Little League.

If that's the way he wants to play it, I'm good with that.

I shake my head sadly. "You know, Bart, it's hard. Really hard to run a restaurant, especially in a competitive place like New York. But we guys have done well. Really well. In fact, we were looking into expanding next door when we got the news about the developer."

Bartlett takes a step back to look at me. "Oh. You were gonna take over Pawsh Pets? Now that's interesting. How'd Livvy feel about that?"

"Oh, she didn't like it. Not at all."

He looks around the room, energized at the possibility of drama.

I knew something was off about this guy.

"You know, Enzo, to get serious for a moment, you really shouldn't have animals in EastSide. It's a health code violation to have pets in a restaurant," he scolds.

"Um, yeah. You're right. But we thought one time would be okay, since it's for a good cause."

He raises his eyebrows at me, not about to let it go. "You need a variance. Or a conditional use permit."

I look at him, trying to assess whether this is a suggestion or a threat.

I nod. "You're right," I concede to keep the peace.

"I'd hate to see you get cited by the health department, especially when your hold on the place is so tenuous."

Um, what?

He waves at someone across the room, and after a shoulder cuff, wanders off.

I stand there with my mouth open.

18

ENZO

Two hours later, with all the guests gone, Livvy kicks her shoes off and plops her feet up on a chair in the dining room. The cleaning crew is buzzing around us, eager to get home, so we move to a far corner where we can all chat privately.

"Wow. That was a hit," Livvy says. "Wine & Whiskers was a success. There's no doubt we have the support of the community. Even Bartlett came. With that *wife* of his." She fake-gags.

Definitely something there, between Livvy and the wife. I'll dig into that later.

"I only got to say hi to him," Owen says, setting a brown shopping bag in the middle of our table and plopping his ass down next to Livvy. Like, really close to Livvy.

He pulls out a Bud Lite and passes the first one to her.

She snorts. "*You* drink Bud Lite?" She drops her head back and laughs, and I know it's cheesy as hell, but it sounds like music.

Dammit. I don't want to like her. At least not *that* way. We may have a very contentious time ahead of us where we all have to make difficult decisions. My loyalty, of course, is to EastSide. It's possible things could get ugly.

But sitting here, trying not to stare at her bare legs propped up on a chair, giving me the slightest peek at her smooth thighs, has me thinking with my little head more than I should.

And Owen's cockblocking me is not making me happy.

He clinks beer bottles with Livvy and the rest of us. "Yes, yes, I do drink Bud Lite, Livvy. I'm not *that* fancy. Geez."

She rolls her eyes. It's funny, seeing her so relaxed and casual.

And I thought she couldn't stand us guys. What changed? Or were we wrong all along?

"The party was a great success," Owen says. "We had a good turnout and people were psyched to be here with their pets."

I raise a finger. "Not everyone was thrilled with the

pet theme, or with the attendance of our four-legged friends."

All eyes turn my way.

"What? What do you mean?" Owen asks.

"Yeah. Did someone say something?" Livvy asks.

I think carefully about what I'm going to say. I don't want to create a mountain out of a mole hill. Maybe Bartlett's remark was nothing more than a casual joke. But something's telling me it wasn't.

"It was weird, but I was chatting with Bart Murray, you know, probing him for info about the mysterious developer, and he changed the subject to say we aren't supposed to have animals in here."

Owen's mouth drops. "Really?"

"I know. Well, I agreed and laughed it off, explaining it was a one-time thing. And then he said something about how it would be bad to get a citation from the health department when we are about to head into a period of uncertainty."

"Are you *kidding*?" Weston sets his beer down.

They're quiet while they digest this bit of information.

Personally, I'm not surprised. There's something off about Bartlett, beyond his cheesy politician-type glad-handing. He's smarmy, sure, but there's another thing bothering me. I think I know what it is.

I know people like Bartlett Murray. I grew up surrounded by them. People who smile in your face one day and stab you in the back the next. I'm from a scrappy neighborhood, and people do what they have to in order to get by. Does that excuse them? Depends on who you ask.

It's the way things are done in some places. Don't like something the city does? 'Encourage' a local council person to change things up.

And that encouragement usually comes in the form of dollars. My father always told me that's how things were done in the old country, and those traditions followed people here. He saw nothing wrong with it, even when he learned most of America didn't operate that way.

Pops wanted the landscaping contract for all the local parks? He 'talked' to someone who could help, and they did. Don't know how much it cost him, but he got what he wanted.

I can smell that shit a mile away.

"I have a weird feeling Bartlett is up to something. I don't know why he'd bother with a veiled threat, though. I thought he liked us. We've certainly given him enough free drinks."

Weston gets to his feet. "Yeah, the guy's a major mooch. Hey, I have to close out some things in the office. If you leave before me, be sure to lock up."

Interesting. Looks like I'm the only one tripping about Bartlett's odd comment. Owen's barely listening, in fact.

I quickly figure out why. And what he has in mind

is a lot more fun than worrying about a creepy city councilperson.

Livvy pulls her shoes back on. "I need to get going too. I have an early grooming appointment with Mrs. Perkin's dog. "You know, the one that—"

I raise my hands. "Yeah, yeah. I remember that canine beast. Look at you, living the good life."

She sticks her tongue out at me. "A girl's gotta do what a girl's gotta do," she sing-songs.

Damn. Is she flirting? Livvy, of the sensible shoes, vegetarian tastes, and verbal diarrhea?

I like it. And so does my cock.

She gets to her feet, but Owen grabs her hand.

"Admit it. We put on a hell of a party, Liv," he says.

Damn. We're doing nicknames now?

She giggles. Actually giggles. Then, she goes all high school on us by bending down and laying one right on Owen's lips.

And just like a high schooler, she straightens back up and tosses her hair around. The full theatrical package.

Was she like this in high school?

No. No way. I'd bet the restaurant and everything else I own that she was the quiet nerd in the corner, plotting her getaway.

How do I know this? I watched girls like her. I wanted to get to know them better. But my dumb-ass jock friends would have reamed me for going after any girl other than the 'populars.' Fuck, how I hated that time in my life. I was trapped. Didn't know how to get out. Until graduation rolled around and I said so long to those douchebags.

And now, finally, I have a sexy, nerdy girl right in front of me, only she just kissed my goddamn friend.

While these thoughts linger, a hot knot of jealousy twists my gut, and the smoked abalone I had for dinner is suddenly backfiring on me. How the hell did I become a jealous little bitch? Hell, I've had more love interests than Mrs. Perkins's beast has taken dumps. And yet.

I'm still irate.

Whatever. I'm not giving up that easily.

I lean back in my chair, all Steve McQueen-cool and shit. "Damn, Livvy. What about me?"

This could work out well. Or crash and burn.

She looks me up and down like some kind of seductress.

My God, her constant surprises are some of the most erotic things I've ever seen.

And *this* is why I have a thing for hot nerds. Granted, she just kissed my jerk friend, but the unexpected nature of it is fucking hot.

"Oh, Enzo. You feeling a little left out?" she laughs, like a bell tinkling in the breeze.

I have to swallow before I speak so my voice doesn't crack like some kind of horny high school virgin. "Well, yeah. What the hell, Livvy?" I say in a voice a couple octaves lower than normal.

Owen snorts. Asshole.

But it doesn't matter. All that does is that the lovely Livvy saunters over to me, bends down, giving me a nice view of her cleavage, and plants a full-lipped kiss on me, lingering there for a second or two, just like I hoped she would.

Fuck yeah.

While our lips are joined, I guide her to my lap and weave my fingers through her hair, pulling her to me. I've wanted this all damn night, and I'm not letting her get away now.

Fuck Owen and everybody else.

Although he doesn't seem to mind. I catch him out of the corner of my eye, smiling and nodding.

"You're fucking beautiful," I whisper.

I run a hand up her thigh and she explodes in goosebumps. I continue to her ass cheek, where she's so smooth and warm that I have to pause there, caressing her soft bum.

She turns, and damn if Owen hasn't made his way over to us to get in on the action. She tilts her face to kiss him, and while she does, still in my lap and hanging on to me, I reach inside her gaping dress to see the breasts I'd been getting peeks of all night long.

Seriously. This woman holds no end of surprises. She's sexy and has no damn idea.

She sighs into Owen's mouth, and my fingers continue up her inner thigh. She shivers at the light touch and I am not fucking kidding, parts her legs for me when I brush the thin strip of panty covering her pussy. She shifts her hips to press into my hand, and we're done with this freaking awkward position.

I lift her to her feet, and one look at Owen tells me he's on the same page. I lay her back on the white tablecloth, scooting her ass to the edge. That's when I push her legs up on my shoulders and press my face into her.

And I'll be damned if she doesn't shimmy her hips and pull aside the crotch of her panties for me.

Holy shit.

I cup her pussy and let one, then two fingers, slide inside her. She arches her back and bucks her head and I've got a bonafide little sex goddess on my hands.

Our hands, I should say. At the other end of the table, Owen's kissing her neck while reaching inside her dress to play with her beautiful tits.

She clenches around my fingers and I am a man obsessed. I want to see her come, to feel her writhe under me as she surrenders.

I want to come too, and my cock is aching inside my pants, painfully constrained, but staying put for the time being.

"Oh God," she whimpers. "Yes, yes, like that."

While I finger-fuck her, I lower myself to her clit, which I swipe at with my tongue. After a few torturous lashes, I gently pull her hard bud between my lips. She arches up into my face and shudders with a cry.

"That's it, baby," Owen murmurs, "you come all over Enzo's face like a good girl."

She thrashes under me so hard I have to wrap my arms around her thighs, her moans increasing, everything about her burning hot, and I witness one of the most beautiful fucking things I've ever seen.

I move Owen aside and lay a kiss on her mouth so she can taste herself, and she laps at me like a hungry little kitten, savoring her sexiness just like I did.

Goddamn, am I in trouble.

"Oh my God," she says when she's ready to come up for air.

She pushes herself up on her elbows and blinks, looking around like she's lost.

I'll take that as a good sign.

"What did you guys just do to me?" she laughs.

We help put her back together and when she wobbles to her feet, I hold her shoes as she steps into them.

She covers her mouth as she yawns. "Oh my gosh. Sorry about that, I'm so rude. It's been a day, hasn't it?"

"And a night too," Owen adds.

"Can I walk you home?" I ask.

She straightens up. "No. That's okay. I'll have my pepper spray and stun gun, one in each hand.

Jesus Christ. She's deadly.

"C'mon," Owen says. "We can't let you walk home by yourself."

She puts a hand on the side of his cheek and, as if he

can't help himself, he turns into her palm to kiss it. "It's okay. Really. You guys have stuff to do yet. I'll be fine. It's a safe neighborhood."

Well, damn. It's hard to argue with that. But I still feel like a major douche, letting her walk home alone, especially after what we just did.

She kisses Owen and then me. "G'night, guys. Tell Weston he missed a good time."

She giggles and heads for the door, and Owen and I watch her walk off into the night.

"Jesus," Owen says, "she's gonna kill someone."

She already kind of did.

19

LIVVY

"THANKS," I call after the mailman.

What I really want to say is 'fuck you very much' for dropping off a new stack of bills. But hell, it's not his fault he's the bearer of bad news.

It's mine. All mine. There's no one else to blame.

But as if he's channeling me, Harry hisses at him before he leaves.

I decide to open my credit card bill first. Get the worst pain out of the way.

And painful is a good way to describe it. Not only have I maxed out my credit limit, I've also exceeded it, and right there in red, like a flashing neon 'loser' sign, is a juicy penalty for my overspending.

Last night's zesty fun aside, I wonder if the bistro

boys coming to see me about taking over my space was some kind of sign. And with a developer breathing down our neck, was that the confirmation I needed? Is the universe telling me to pack it in? Abandon ship like the sneaky people across the street who left behind unpaid bills and no forwarding address?

I could be as shitty as them.

But that's not my style.

If Pawsh Pets is not destined for the harsh world of New York retail, I'll go out with guns blazing and debt up to my eyeballs. They'll have to literally drag me from here.

Which looks increasingly likely as evidenced by the pile of financial doom looming before me, like some sort of predetermined death sentence.

Before throwing in the towel, whether for the bistro boys next door or the soulless developer looking to cast me aside, I do have options.

Well, op*tion*. As in *one*. *Not* plural.

My brother-in-law, Carter, otherwise known as one half of the duo Kritter.

Nothing would make him happier than having power over his wife's loser sister, the one with her head in the clouds and not an ounce of sense.

Yes, he said that about me. Krista told me.

Mr. I-know-all-about-business-because-I-wear-a-suit-and-tie would love for me to come begging for money and advice. In fact, I think he's still bitter I didn't come to him for help when I first opened Pawsh

Pets. I certainly don't know everything, but I prefer to muscle through making a few mistakes here and there than have someone breathing down my neck, especially when he thinks Pawsh Pets was a stupid idea, anyway.

His superiority complex reaches into every aspect of his life, and certainly doesn't need any more feeding, especially not by the likes of me. It's already a struggle to keep my spirits up on days like today without having him rub my failures in my face. Plus, with great satisfaction, I have no doubt he'll tell everyone.

He'll be especially vicious since I blew off his friend.

Yeah, no. My brother-in-law is no more an option for bankrolling my business than the homeless man down the street. Difference is, the homeless guy is way nicer.

The doorbell jingles and I look up to see Jewel fly in.

"Oh my god, I'm so sorry. My crystal healing class went over. I told the teacher I needed to bolt, but she just said do I want my energy field balanced or not." She looks at me, clearly powerless in the face of such a challenge, and shrugs.

"Oh yeah. Must get the energy fields balanced," I say.

I have no idea what she means and I'm not asking, although it's likely she'll tell me anyway. I slide the mail into my apron pocket for the time being, where I can forget about it, if just for a little while.

Jewel grabs the seat behind the cash wrap counter, and fiddles with a bowl of little cat collars. "So…" she draws out, "how was the *partay*? Sorry I had to leave early."

I wave away her concerns. It would have been great had she stayed, but it was a big day at her past life regression therapy course and I could see she was exhausted by it. Or was it her alien abduction meridian tapping class? Hard to keep them straight.

"It was good. Big turnout, the animals were all cute and well-behaved. I think we got the attention of the neighborhood, that's for sure."

She doesn't need to know how the evening ended.

She gives me a sly look. "I bet that's not all the attention you got."

Oh no. Does she know?

I raise my eyebrows. "What are you getting at?"

I need to know.

She looks around like she has a big secret. "The guys. *The EastSide guys.*"

I keep my expression neutral, but the feeling of being a kid and getting caught doing something naughty washes over me. My face heats and I want to run back to my office even though it's where the rest of Pawsh's outstanding bills are stored.

She slams her hand on the counter. "Fuck yeah. I knew it. They like you, Livvy."

Oh my god. They do not.

Last night was a fluke. A one-time thing. We were

buzzed and in the mood to celebrate a successful party. Those guys are as interested in me as Harry is in being a lap cat.

Jewel is just being… silly.

I roll my eyes and shake my head, maybe a bit too vigorously. But it's the best defense I can come up with at the moment. I should have been better prepared. Of course she's going to have nosy questions.

She leans toward me, her homemade body oil stinging my nose. "Livvy, listen to me," she says, taking my hand. "I was *there*. I *saw* it. They can't keep their eyes off you."

"Shhhh. They're right next door," I say, gesturing at our shared wall.

She rolls her eyes, then drops her head back and groans. The drama must serve her well in her acting classes. "Jesus. You really have no idea? C'mon."

She walks around the counter and gets right in my face. "You're blushing, Olive-also-known-as-Livvy Fontaine. You're red as a beet, girlfriend. And there's something you're not telling meee," she sings, wagging a finger in my face.

I avoid her gaze by straightening up some cat treats that don't need straightening. "Jewel, there's nothing to tell," I say, my voice squeaking through the lie.

Dammit. I'm not cut out to lie. I'm just not.

"Oh my God, there *is*. Tell me, Livvy, or I'll… I don't know… I'll go over there and bring back one of those weird-ass guinea hens they have on the menu. I'll eat it in front of you, then throw the carcass in your office garbage can. Skin, bones, gristle. The whole thing."

Now that's a low blow. She's not fighting fair.

"You can't afford one of their hens, or whatever is it."

She smirks. "You're right, I can't. But with Dad's AmEx, I can. You never know when you're going to need an emergency guinea hen. He'll understand."

I happen to know Jewel's 'emergency AmEx' is not used exclusively for emergencies. Her agreement with her father is none of my business, but I'm pretty sure Dad pays for her wacky courses and who knows what else.

"Very funny, bringing meat here. You'd never do that."

She looks at me very intently. "Oh yes, I would. So, spill. What happened?"

I roll my shoulders to fend off the growing tension and look out the front window, because I can't bear to see Jewel's face when she finds out I kissed two guys.

I hold my hands up. I surrender. "Fine, fine. You're right, something happened. But it's *so* not a big deal."

Yeah, right. It's so not a big deal I that stayed up half the night thinking about it with a smile on my face. I was only able to sleep after a date with BOB.

Battery-operated-boyfriend.

I am still avoiding Jewel's gaze. But it's time to come clean. "I kissed them," I mumble.

This should hopefully feed her relentless interest.

"*What?*" she screeches.

I back up, my hands over my ears. "Ouch Jewel, that was freaking loud. Anyway, you heard me. There's nothing else to say." I head to the back of the store to clean up the dog-grooming station. I have one or two pups coming in today. I can't remember for sure.

My mind is a little muddled.

Not satisfied, Jewel jumps in front of me.

"What? What do you want now?" I huff.

She points a finger right into my chest, something an employee should probably never do. But I let her get away with all kinds of shit because I'm a pushover that way.

Plus, I like her. We're friends.

"Tell. Me. Now." She purses her lips and narrows her eyes, like I'm supposed to be afraid.

Instead, I'm annoyed, and at the same time, tickled. I didn't realize how much fun recounting the evening would be. I liked it, being with them. I'm not going to lie. I want it to happen again.

I sigh deeply, finally defeated. "I kissed Owen and Enzo. Wes was up in his office. And we did... other stuff."

The *woo-hoo* that came out of Jewel's mouth was probably heard down the street and even around the block. Harry got up from his perch and meowed at us before running into the closet.

I want to explain to Jewel it was just a silly whim, it meant nothing, and will never happen again. That I'd had one too many glasses of unfiltered, organic champagne, and that I'd be extra careful next time.

If there ever is a next time.

Those guys aren't interested in me. I hold no promise or potential of being the better half of a New York 'power couple.' People who own shops like me don't make it into the glamorous side of city life. For heaven's sake, I wash dogs and express their anal glands.

I'm fine with that. I am perfectly happy with my lot in life—my little business, my little apartment, and my little circle of friends. I really, truly, do not want or need anything else.

That's why the notion of losing Pawsh Pets has kept me up at night, led me to drinking one glass of champagne too many, and gave me the guts to mess around two gorgeous men, the likes of whom I am sure I'll never kiss again.

I did it without thinking, with no concern for consequences, and I'd do it again if I had the chance.

20

LIVVY

By the time Jewel settles down, the smells of food cooking next door are pouring into Pawsh, flicking me with reminders of how gorgeous and sexy the bistro boys are. It's like I'm walking down the street wanting to be left alone and some annoying person keeps tapping me on the shoulder, wanting my attention.

I don't want to smell their food. I don't want to be thinking of them.

Leave me alone!

I need to get it together. I know I have options. There are always options. I could sell a kidney. I mean, hell, I have two so can surely spare one. Or I could sell my soul, because at the end of all this, what will I need that for, anyway?

Whichever sells for the most on the black market, of course.

I slink back to my office, needing a moment. Pawsh Pets will be fine, I chant to myself. Hadn't Jewel told me about one of her classes, the manifesting one on the law of attraction? I fish through my desk for the list of affirmations she gave me.

The universe conspires to give me everything I desire.

I am a magnet for wealth and abundance.

I believe in myself and my abilities.

There are more on the list, but I like these best and besides, I only have so much time for this stuff.

I sit for a moment, waiting for the universe to rain riches and other good things down on me before I realize it probably doesn't happen this fast. No, I must be patient. It says so at the bottom of the instruction page.

The front bell tinkles and I stick my head out of the office.

Arthur's here.

"Hey, honey," he says to Jewel as they air kiss. "Damn, your hair looks fierce. Oh, to be your age again," he sighs.

"Arthur!" I run to hug him, and he looks as surprised as I am. I'm not a hugger, but for some reason I really need one right now.

He clasps his hands together. "So," he says playfully, "tell me everything. I know you've been to a couple parties next door. How'd they go?"

Jewel taps her chin with her finger. "First things first. Where were *you* last night, Arthur? We missed you."

He looks down and shuffles his feet. "I, um, well, I had a last-minute Grindr date. Sorry I missed the festivities. But you know I am a big supporter of Pawsh Pets."

I want to ask how his date went, but something tells me not to.

Instead, Jewel jumps out of her seat. "Arthur, seeing as you asked, Livvy *does* have something to share," she says with an evil glint.

Oh for cripe's sake. "Jewel, really?" I cry.

Arthur cuts me off, grabbing my forearms with a death grip. "Tell me!" he shrieks.

"Arthur, you're hurting me—"

"She kissed the guys next door," Jewel blurts.

Arthur drops my arms and takes a step back, staring at me with wide eyes and an open mouth. "Oh… my…" he says after a minute, his eyes tearing up.

Is he for real?

I think I've landed on an alien planet where all the people are crazy and I'm the only normal one, which isn't good, because that means, when it comes down to it, I am the odd one out. The true weirdo. Even though I am actually, truly normal.

"My dear Livvy," Arthur says, wiping at a tear. "I'm so… so happy for you. I… I knew you had it in you." His voice breaks up.

Oh my God.

"You both need to chill the hell out. It was a one-time thing and it won't happen again."

Arthur's head snaps back. "And why not?"

I shrug. "I'm not their type. And I don't like them anyway."

Okay, no one's going to believe that lie, least of all Jewel and Arthur.

"Why?" he snaps. "What do you mean you're *not their type*? Have you looked in the mirror lately? You're gorgeous, my girl."

Jewel nods in agreement, and I wonder if they've both been consuming edibles this afternoon.

"Whatever, you guys," I say, waving my hand.

They look at each other and I know I'm about to be ganged up on. I brace myself.

"Livvy, you've got gorgeous blonde curls, long legs, a great ass, and if I do say so myself, nice tits," he says.

Oh my God. My tits again?

"I think you're crazy but thank you all the same. You are true friends."

Arthur brings his hands up to the sides of his face. "You know how I get *feelings* about things?" With air quotes around 'feelings', he turns to Jewel. "You know this about me, right?"

She nods enthusiastically. "Absolutely."

They once took a course together on following their intuition to illuminate one's path in life. Or something like that.

Arthur takes my hand in both of his. "It will happen again, honey. I know it."

His phone buzzes and he drops my hand. "Oh, well, look at that. I gotta run, ladies. Kisses!" He heads for the door like his ass is on fire.

"Hey, where are you going? You know my secret now. What about yours?" I call after him.

He smiles at me like I'm an idiot. "Some girls keep their secrets." He blows me a kiss and is off.

Funny guy, that Arthur, thinking the bistro boys would be interested in me.

As the day draws to a close, and Jewel is off for another of her classes, I'm inhaling the scents of mouthwatering rosemary and garlic from next door. I'm thinking ahead to what I'll have for dinner. Maybe noodles from the Chinese place down the street.

Then a text comes in.

Liv. Hey

Hello?

Its Owen. Yes, I have your number

My stomach somersaults. I don't like it.

I'll ask how you got my number later

C'mon over. We'll make you some veggies

Oh my God. He's inviting me over. Like to hang out. Spend time together. Eat food.

Give me 5

21

LIVVY

Before I left this morning, I *just so happened* to slip some bronzer and lip gloss in my bag, so I stand in front of the cracked hand mirror hanging in my closet-slash-office and get to work. Not because I care to impress the guys. It's just that it's been a busy day and I might appear a little… tired.

I look at myself from as many angles as I can muster in the small mirror and lousy lighting. I want to use enough makeup to liven myself up, but not so much it looks like I'm trying hard.

Or trying at all.

Ugh. Who am I trying to fool? I've never been a cool girl, and I certainly haven't turned into one overnight.

Even if I did mess around with two gorgeous guys less than twenty-four hours ago.

I adjust my boobs to give them the desired *oomph,* make sure I don't have a wedgie, and leave for the day after I've fed the grumpy cat. I hesitate outside Pawsh Pets for a minute while I mentally collect a few topics of potential conversation, in case I get tongue-tied. I read an article about this recently, successfully making non-boring small talk, in *Glisten Magazine,* my favorite publication in the world. It's best to be prepared.

Have you ever tried strawberries on pizza?

Did you know some people can peel bananas with their feet?

What's the most embarrassing thing that's ever happened to you?

Okay, that last one is a tired old standby, but the article says it works like a charm if you absolutely, positively, run out of things to say.

Convinced I'm ready, or as ready as I'll ever be, I walk the last few steps to EastSide, and saunter in like I was invited there.

Which I was.

Be cool. Be cool.

Owen is at my side in seconds, which makes my heart jump like the idiot I am. I'm sure these guys are only being nice to me so they can snag my store if and when we manage to fend off the evil developer.

But I can enjoy the attention while it lasts, right?

He places a soft hand on my upper arm and for a

moment it seems like he's going to kiss me or something. But he stops and pulls back. It's all good though, because he flashes me that mega-watt smile, and if that's all I get from him for the rest of my life, that will be okay.

He ushers me over to a small table with a nice view of the entire restaurant. "This is the table we reserve for special guests."

I shake my head. "Oh no, I don't have to sit here. You can give me a seat by the bathroom in the back. Please don't fuss over me."

"We're not fussing. We are treating you the way you deserve to be treated."

Huh. No idea what that means. Maybe they're angling for more nooky? Would that be such a bad thing? I sit my ass in the chair Owen's pulled out for me, and before I can say another thing, Enzo's motoring toward me with a plate of something red.

Dark red. Like blood red.

Shit. Have they forgotten I'm a vegetarian? And even more important, if they do set down a plate of bloody meat in front of me, I can't promise I won't vomit all over it.

As it is, some of the smells here are a challenge for my stomach. But I take a sip of the biodynamic wine Owen's served me, made with, as he explained, some kind of manure, and marvel at how good it is and how it doesn't smell like cow shit at all.

I am clearly putting my life on the line with these

guys. But none of their diners have keeled over dead yet, at least not that I'm aware of.

Enzo drops a plate before me and steps back, beaming. "Hey, gorgeous."

Okay. Now I don't care what's on the damn plate. They could serve me grasshoppers, and this would be one of the best nights of my life.

I manage to tear my gaze away from Enzo's dark eyes, the ones that make me want to take my clothes off even though I'm in a crowded restaurant, as the scent of something so delicious wafts up it brings tears to my eyes.

"It's called beet tartare," he says. "Let me know what you think. It's somewhat of an experiment. I'd like to add it to the menu."

Beet tartare. Clever.

Before me are shavings of my favorite root vegetable so thin I can almost see through them, surrounded by capers and shallots, with a tiny crust of bread on one side, and what I'm pretty sure is a blob of goat cheese on the other.

My mouth waters. The dish smells like heaven and looks even prettier. I look up at the guys in awe. "How did you know I love beets?"

Enzo shrugs. "I didn't, darlin'. But hey, I gotta get back to the kitchen." He turns, and as he retreats, I see his chef jacket is just short enough to show off his ass, perfectly covered by a pair of faded blue jeans.

Catching me staring, Owen's amused, and gives me

a little bow. "I have to get back to work too. Enjoy the dish and give me a wave if you need anything."

I dive into my beets, using all the strength I can muster not to inhale the delicately flavored vegetables. In fact, I force myself to set my fork down in between bites to avoid humiliating myself.

The restaurant is filling up and the light buzz of socializing people and the quiet clatter of dishes bounce off the white wall in front of me and back to the brick wall behind me, where it seems to sink in the way a sponge mops up water.

How do they do that? I look around EastSide, really look around, and realize the other couple times I've been here I was distracted by people and my anxiety, and not paid any attention to how simple but elegant it is.

The lighting is made of what looks like repurposed industrial materials, lending a scruffy-chic feel, while the chairs and banquettes are covered in crackly leather upholstery, the kind you might find on an easy chair in an old-school men's club.

The funny thing is, it's not overly masculine or stuffy, thanks to the huge paintings of chickens on the far wall. They lend just enough whimsy, as if their job is to remind everyone not to take themselves too seriously.

Separately, all these components might be weird. Together they are perfect.

"Hey. Looks like you enjoyed that wine."

I look up to find Weston standing over me, his dress shirt sleeves rolled up far enough to show his very muscular forearms.

Damn him.

I look at my empty glass and realize how fast I sucked down my wine. "Busted. It was so good. And to think, it doesn't taste like manure at all."

He drops his head back and laughs. "I can just imagine what Owen told you. It's not made with manure. It's just something they put on the vineyard with a mixture of other stuff."

Same thing, if you ask me.

"Let me get you another," he says.

Holy shit. I could get used to being waited on hand and foot.

When he returns, I motion for him to take the seat opposite me. "Weston, tell me, why are you guys doing this for me?"

Fuck. Did that sound ungrateful?

The corner of his mouth crooks up as he leans an elbow on the table. "You brought all those people to the restaurant last night. We want to show our appreciation and do something nice for you."

I open my mouth to speak, but his blue eyes are too damn distracting to keep my shit together. So, I take a sip of my wine and sit back in my seat like I'm a cool girl and do stuff like this all the time.

I can finally formulate a thought when his knee brushes mine under the table.

Ohmygod. Was that intentional?

No. No way.

He's got long legs just like I do. People like us bump into stuff all the time.

Then it happens again. I decide to handle it the way I do everything else.

By putting my foot in my mouth.

"Weston," I say slowly so I can keep it together, "did you just brush my knee on purpose? Or are you just super clumsy?"

Of course, he has the perfect comeback. "Well, it depends, Livvy. It depends on whether you liked it or not. If you did, then yes, it was on purpose. If you didn't, I'll swear it was an accident and never do it again."

Damn him. Men like him always know what to say.

I scoop the last sliver of beet off my plate and savor it, letting the earthy taste dissolve on my tongue. As long as there's food in my mouth, he can't possibly expect me to answer.

Right?

I swallow and reach for a sip of water because I don't know what else to do.

And yet, he never breaks our gaze.

"It's fine," I say in a choked voice. "You're not bothering me."

He slaps his hand on the table. "Okay, then. I haven't pissed you off. At least not yet."

Um, piss me off? Like that's even possible.

While I'm trying my best to come up with something equally witty, which is a stupid waste of time, Enzo returns. I have no idea what he's bringing my way, and not even after he sets it down in front of me.

"Hey, Wes," he says, clapping his buddy on the back.

Weston gets to his feet and pushes his chair in. Disappointment washes over me, but I remind myself to get it together.

He's not my freaking date. He's just being cordial.

"Would you look at that," he says as Enzo sets the plate before me.

I don't know what this is, but it smells like pure heaven.

"This, Livvy, is a roasted cauliflower steak with Romanesco sauce and almonds."

Cauliflower steak?

"Wow," I say, reaching for my fork and knife even though both guys are still standing there.

I should probably wait for them to depart, but nothing's stopping me from trying this beautiful creation.

I pop a bite into my mouth and moan even though I don't mean to. My eyes fall closed as my tastebuds explode with happiness.

"I think she likes it, Wes."

"Hmmm. I'm not so sure."

My eyes fly open. "Are you kidding? I would marry that stuff, that's how much I love it."

They laugh and head back to work.

Good lord. What have I gotten myself into?

The food's amazing. The guys are amazing.

But if I had to choose one over the other, I might opt for the food.

Kidding.

I continue eating and drinking until I have a stomachache, the guys plying me with dishes like celery root 'scallops,' which are not actually scallops, and a vegan 'foie gras,' which of course is not foie gras, either.

Did they really prepare this stuff just for me? I mean, it's not like they threw some broccoli in the steamer and called it a day like most people do when feeding vegetarians. These dishes are complicated. Clearly, time and effort went into them. A lot.

If they're thinking the way to this woman's heart is through her stomach, they are right.

The question is, why? Hell, we've had our businesses next door to each other for two years and barely exchanged a word except for Owen, who buys things for his supposed mother's cat.

He must think I'm an idiot. Dude, just admit you have a cat.

But it's when the guys bring me dessert, a chai molten-chocolate cake with vegan whipped cream on the side, that I lose my mind. I don't care what their ulterior motives are, if they even have any. I'm going to enjoy this moment—food that's out of this world, and the attention of three beautiful men, and worry about what they might be up to some other damn time.

22

OWEN

"I'M THINKING YOU LIKE THAT."

I point my chin in the direction of the plate currently in front of Livvy.

She stops wolfing down her dessert for a moment, a smudge of chocolate on her upper lip. Which I have no intention of telling her about.

I prefer to imagine wiping it off with the corner of my napkin, and then, if anything's left…

Down, boy.

With the restaurant mostly empty after a successful dinner service, the other guys pull up chairs to the table where our lovely guest has been camping out all night.

She ignores my tease and finishes the last of her

cake, then stares at the plate with genuine sadness now that it's gone. The only thing left is to pick up the dish and start licking it. But even in her state of dessert heaven, she seems to know this would be inappropriate, at least in public.

She smiles. "I don't even... you guys. That cake was... fucking awesome." She finally brings a napkin to her lips and dabs away the spot of chocolate.

Dammit.

Enzo runs his finger through what's left. "Livvy, I think you missed a dab of whipped cream," he teases, waving his finger around in front of her face.

She puts her hands up. "Hey, cut that out."

But Enzo wipes the dab of it on her nose, which she looks at with crossed eyes.

"I'm sure I'm a sight," she says in a squeaky voice.

Most women I know would lose their shit if someone put food on their face. She scoops the dab of whipped cream off her nose and plops it into her mouth.

Damn. I wanted to do that.

"Thank you," she says, sitting back in the banquette and rubbing her belly, which is, admittedly, a little bigger than when she came in this evening. "I've never had anything like this. Unbelievable."

This is part of what I like about this woman. Not the big belly per se, but that she doesn't hide that she enjoys food, even to the point where her tummy protrudes like it does for all of us after a big meal.

Too many Manhattan women would pretend there weren't hungry or didn't like the food before they'd allow their stomachs to stick out even the tiniest bit.

Livvy lets it all hang out. And it's sexy. Not that she doesn't take care of herself—she's always well-put together even if she is wearing socks with her Birkenstocks—it's just that she knows where to stop. She doesn't have the blown-up fish lips so many women do, nor the blank stare the same ones get from too much Botox.

She's real. And natural.

I never knew how hot that was.

Enzo's waving his finger in her face again, this time with the last crumb from her dessert plate. She parts her lips and wraps them around the last taste of dessert so quickly she looks like a lizard catching a fly.

Except, she doesn't let his finger go, instead letting the last morsel of chocolate wash through her mouth, not missing a single tastebud. She closes her eyes as she swallows.

I try to swallow too, but my mouth is too dry.

Enzo pushes his finger in a little further.

Goddamn him. Cock-blocked again.

He looks at Weston and me. "She liked the dessert, guys, and she likes this even better." He twists his finger between her lips and pulses it in a way she'll either think is sexy as hell or the most vulgar thing that's ever happened to her.

I'm thinking she'll go with the latter, but when she

snort-laughs, relief washes over me. All we need is to mortally offend this woman just when we're making some progress on our developing friendship.

Weston elbows Enzo out of the way and moves closer to Livvy, so close their mouths are nearly touching, which they finally do when he buries her lips in his. One of her hands is on the side of his face, the other splayed on the table, her fingers flexing and opening, her nails digging into the wood beneath them.

I scoot around the other side of the banquette to sandwich her, and when she realizes I'm there, she shocks the shit out of me by breaking with Weston and kissing me. I glance around to see if anyone in the restaurant is enjoying the show, but the only people left are back in the kitchen, banging things around.

Looks like we have a wild child on our hands again. Wonders never cease, and all that shit.

While Livvy is being tag-teamed, Enzo lowers the lights. Votive candles, continuing to flicker on the tables, give the room a twinkly effect with just enough light thrown on Livvy and the guys to present a scene that is sexy as fuck. I unbutton her blouse, revealing a lacy bra holding the nicely rounded breasts I'd enjoyed the night before. Weston goes after her neck while she's turned toward me, and she moans lightly, giving me a huge fucking hard-on that I may have to rub out in the men's room.

Livvy comes up for air. "Guys, my apartment is just a few blocks away."

"Mine's even closer," I pipe up.

She raises an eyebrow. "How do you know where I live?"

"I've seen you come and go. You think you're the only one who follows people?"

Even in the dim light I see her blush.

"You noticed me in the neighborhood? You follow me?" she asks, incredulous.

"Maybe. I'm not incriminating myself, so that's all I will say."

I'm not a stalker, but of course I've noticed Livvy around, coming and going, as we all do. And I might have followed her to the grocery store once or twice, because she was wearing a spectacularly snug pair of blue jeans. She never had a clue.

But she doesn't need to know that shit.

We waste no time guiding Livvy to her feet. Without another word, I take the restaurant's keys out of my pockets, let everyone out the front door, lock up, and lead the way to my place.

23

OWEN

LIVVY GIGGLES, holding hands with each of the guys as I bring up the rear. They talk and laugh under the street-lights, and a light splatter of rain starts to dampen our hair and clothes—but not our moods. A wet asphalt smell rises from the street, and I think about how far I've come and how much further I'll go if all continues according to plan.

There is one nagging worry. There always is for me. And it's the damn developer who wants us out.

But I'll worry about that tomorrow.

I open the door to my brownstone building, once a single-family home for a rich New York family, but now divided into three units, one on each floor. We begin the climb up, because of course I have the top floor—it's quieter and I have roof access. When we get there, I let everyone in and nudge the guys aside because, dammit, it's my turn to kiss Livvy. My cat Cheddar runs right up to her, and she bends to pet him.

"So cute. I thought you said you didn't have a cat, but your mother did?"

I nod and the guys roll their eyes. "Yeah. Mom is out of town. I'm cat sitting."

Worst lie in the history of lies.

Before she can ask any more questions, I pull her to me, her pillowy lips meeting mine. In seconds her tongue is flicking my lips.

I'm in freaking heaven.

I run my hand over her breasts and continue to unbutton what one of the guys started. I take my time, though, like really take my time, because I don't want to scare her off.

"You're fucking beautiful, you know," I whisper in between kisses.

She pulls back for a moment and looks at me like I'm crazy, then giggles lightly.

Damn. She has no freaking idea.

I lead her to the sofa as Enzo and Weston stand back and watch. As she lowers herself to a seat, I stand before her.

Right before her.

She places her hands on my outer thighs, sliding them until she reaches the cheeks of my ass. There's no doubt she sees the huge bulge behind the fly of my pants, and when she rubs her cheek against the rough fabric, I nearly cream myself right there. Instead, I rock into her face so she knows just how hard she's made me.

She looks up and she's so earnest. She wants to please. I can see that. But what she doesn't know is that every second of being with her is pleasing—actually more than that. Way more than that.

I run my thumb roughly across her lower lip and she doesn't flinch or even move, and in fact, she pushes into me, taking my thumb, her eyes fluttering closed, suggesting she might like a little rough play.

Moving her hands from my ass, I place them on my belt and fly. Without hesitation, she starts unbuckling and unzipping until my hard cock, all veiny and dripping with precum, falls into her hands. She closes her fingers around me and begins to stroke.

Jesus, it's not that it's been that long since I've been with a woman, but I've *never* been with a woman like Livvy, someone with no ulterior motive, who's asking for nothing, expecting nothing, except companionship and fun and maybe something to remember the evening by.

I watch her study my cock like it's the first she's ever held. She takes me into her mouth with all the confidence in the world, like a woman who enjoys the sensuality of giving and getting pleasure.

I can't help but groan loudly when she runs her

tongue over my cockhead and then down one side of my erection and up the other. Without pausing, she takes me in hand and pulls me completely out my pants so she can tongue my balls.

This woman is going to kill me.

I look over my shoulder at the guys, who watch with great interest. They nod my way and by the time I turn back I've forgotten all about them. It seems Livvy has too—she's not deterred by their presence, not one bit.

She's working my balls, winding me all up. With one foot on the edge of the sofa, I hoist myself closer to her so she can take more. She licks, nips, and sucks while stroking me and it's pure heaven, to have a beautiful woman like Livvy on the end of my cock working her magic, getting ready to take my cum.

We don't have to wait long. The rumbling that starts in my balls shoots up my spine. My dick jerks, seeking release and finally finds it, right into the mouth of the lovely girl before me. I hold her hair out of the way and pump between her lips, in and out, until she gags lightly, and triggers the finale to one of the hardest orgasms I've ever had.

I can't help myself when I pull Livvy's head down on me, banging the back of her throat as I unload. She takes it like a champ, and even when I'm done and she has cum running down her chin, she takes the time to lick me dry like I'm some sort of goddamn lollipop.

All I can think about is when can we do this again.

I take Livvy to my bed where we doze off, still partially clothed, and when I wake up the next morning, I rouse her, and go to the living room to find that Enzo and Weston are long gone.

24

OWEN

Lunch service is busy, thank God, because I need something to take my mind off Livvy and that fact that she's only a few feet away on the other side of the kitchen wall, toiling away in her world of pets and their rich owners. Knowing she's so close makes my balls ache, and it's all I can do not to run over there, peek in the window, and run back to the restaurant like a dorky little kid.

She fell asleep last night almost the moment her head hit my pillow, so I wrapped my arms around her and tried to follow suit. It took a while, but I eventually succeeded. For the longest time before I did, I lay awake, smelling her hair, so fresh and clean and not overly perfumed.

God, I sound pussy-whipped.

First chance I get, when the last lunch guest leaves, I run next door.

I need, um, cat food.

Yeah right. Cat food.

I picture the dozens of untouched cans already stored in my pantry and wince. But that doesn't stop me buying more. Hell, they don't go bad. Do they?

"Hi," Livvy says, her eyes lighting up as she leans onto the counter toward me.

Her assistant is nowhere to be found, thank goodness.

If Livvy's embarrassed or bashful about what happened the night before, it's not at all evident. With her hair and makeup all cleaned up, you'd never guess this woman gave me a blowjob last night in front of two of my friends.

It's the quiet ones you have to watch out for, right?

"Hey," I say, looking around the shop, avoiding her gaze while pretending to look for something very important.

For a cat.

Fucking stupid.

Harry, Livvy's in-house mascot, looks up lazily at our conversation, not at all happy at having been disturbed, and with a grunt, goes back to sleep.

"So, Livvy, I need some more of that cat food. For my mom's cat. The one I'm watching. While my mother is out of town."

Sorry, Cheddar. Don't mean to dis you.

Livvy raises an eyebrow. "Does your mom have a zoo or something? How many cats does the woman own?"

She pulls out a shopping basket and walks to the wall, where Cheddar's preferred food is on display and starts piling it in.

"Um, just Cheddar. He eats a lot." I pick up an absurdly overpriced cat treat and a little cat raincoat that says 'Cucci,' which my cat would never wear because, first, he never steps foot outside my apartment and, two, he has way too much pride to dress like a human. I'm buying it anyway.

Livvy eyes the items in the shopping basket and I'm pretty sure she knows the story of the cat belonging to my mother is a bunch of bull.

My mom's *actual* cat? Little thing has been in feline heaven for years.

I watch as Livvy rings up my order. "I'm giving you my friends and family ten percent off."

I raise my hands. "No, no. I didn't come over here hoping for a discount."

She looks at me, her mouth crooked into a smirking half smile. "Then why did you come?"

Okay. Fine. She can see through my cat purchases.

I'm not a sentimental guy. It's well known that I'm a pessimistic pain in the ass. But I have to admit, Livvy has grown on me. Her smart-assed jabs put me right in my place, something most women would never dare to do.

I'm torn between pulling her into my arms and just maintaining our snarky friendship.

My little head gets the better of me. I look around the shop to make sure Livvy's weird assistant isn't around, and take a step closer in order to drop my bomb.

"Liv, are you as attracted to me as I am to you? Because if you are, that would be great. Or terrible. Who knows."

She tilts her head. "I can't believe you need to ask that."

Oh. Right.

I change the subject as quickly as I can. "Hey, I wanted to let you know the guys and I, now that we know we have neighborhood support, have a name for our joint campaign."

Her eyebrows shoot up. "Great. Let's hear it."

"What do you think of 'Operation Don't Tear Down Our Dreams to Build Your Skyscraper'?"

She wrinkles her nose. "It gets right to the point. Although it's… kind of long."

"Yeah, I guess you're right. But we're moving in the right direction, Livvy. The party showed us that the community wants us around. We've won one of the biggest battles."

She nods. "It feels so good. We got way more support than I hoped for."

It hasn't been easy, hashing through options for saving our respective businesses. There've been plenty of times we all wanted to throttle each other, stemming from Weston's initial thoughts of just ignoring it, to spreading rumors and false claims about the developer —Enzo's idea—to my lame approach of going to a community meeting for the sole purpose of beating the shit out of the developer's representatives.

Through all the ridiculous ideas we guys brought to the table, Livvy has been the voice of reason. Our North Star. To put it simply, without her, we'd be pretty much fucked. Thank goodness she's on our team and doesn't completely hate us for trying to buy her business for our own expansion. If this whole developer threat hadn't happened along, I can't imagine what kind of relationship we'd have with her. Would it be spoiled forever as we tried to convince her to sell out to us? Would she hate our fucking guts?

Instead, we're collaborating, not to mention growing on each other, as evidenced by the 'fun' we've been having.

"I know this has been hard on you," I say.

I'm pretty sure it's relief that washes over her face, and for a moment, she's choked up. "It is. It really is, Owen. You have no idea."

I take her hand. "Don't say that Liv. I've been through the ringer. I could tell you stories…"

She tilts her head. "Really? Like what? I thought all

you guys had it so easy. Like anything you want comes your way."

I'm dumbfounded. "Livvy, everyone has challenges. Not a single person walking down the street hasn't been kicked in the teeth once or twice. Or more."

She nods. "I know. You're right. Everyone has shit happen to them. What about you?"

Ugh. I wasn't planning on talking about my life story today… or ever. But here we are.

"My… dad split when I was a kid. Just took off. Mom had to work all the time, so I was basically on my own."

"Wow," she says.

"Yup. Those were hard times. But anyway, know I'm on your side. I want Pawsh Pets to succeed as much as I want EastSide to."

"I feel so lucky, not to be slogging through this by myself. I can't tell you how much it means that you guys have my back. Even if you are carnivores."

"You got me there. But hey, both parties bring something to the table the other needs. It's a win-win, baby."

She gives me a sly look. "I had fun last night," she says quietly.

Yes, she did.

"There's more where that came from," I say.

25

LIVVY

"You know how I have a sixth sense about these things."

I look up from my paperwork at Jewel. Although I love her, this is one of those times I'd really like to strangle her.

"You may as well just tell me. You know I'll figure it out." She presses her lips together like a pissed off kindergarten teacher.

I shake my head and get back to work. Something she should consider doing too. I am so not in the mood.

"You fucked them, didn't you?"

I calmly set my pen down on the cash wrap counter. She's not going to give up until she gets some dirt.

"Jewel, I did not fuck them. I messed around with one of them. With the other two watching," I say as if people do stuff like that all the time.

Maybe they do, and I'm just late to the party. Better late than never, right?

She slams her hand on the counter, scaring the shit out of both Harry and me. The cat takes off for cover by crawling under a low shelf. I wish I could join him.

"I knew you had that level of dirty girl in you, Livvy. You little ho-bag."

I say nothing but get back to filling out an order for more cat beds. After last week's party at EastSide, business picked up a little. Or are the new sales attributable to the cards I handed out at their investor party?

Either way, I am not complaining.

"Are you gonna do it again?" she asks.

I sigh. "I don't know, Jewel. Probably not. It was just something that happened on a whim. Not a lot of thought went into it."

"That's what you think."

"What does that mean?"

She shrugs. "They like you, Livvy. I'm telling you. I know this."

Okay. Fine. They like me. I like them too.

So what?

It's not like I'm going to date the three of them. It's not like I'm going to marry the three of them.

"I'll tell you, Jewel, my top priority right now is to keep Pawsh Pets open. If I get some nooky on the side, that's great. But I don't know what's going to happen to the shop."

She runs this thought through her head until it dawns on her that if Pawsh goes down, that means no more cushy job for her.

Sometimes it takes her a while.

Sure, Jewel can get any number of jobs in the city. But there aren't many where you can come and go, *and* bug your boss about her sex life.

Jewel doesn't know what her future looks like. Neither do I. It doesn't feel good. All I've worked so hard for could be gone overnight if the developers win. And if we do defeat them, does that mean the guys will go right back to trying to buy me out so they can expand?

Am I fucked, either way?

It's the worst, feeling like everyone is out for themselves with no regard for what I want. Sure, I might have messed around with the guys, but does that mean, given the chance, that they wouldn't run me over for their own purposes? Giving someone a blow job does not exactly guarantee they're on your side for life.

Not that that's the reason I did it.

Owen did say we're all one team. But things change. People change.

"I know you're under a lot of stress, Livvy," Jewel says guiltily.

Finally. Someone cutting me a break.

She wrings her hands. "I know I'm a pain in the butt

sometimes, but I do want to help you whatever way I can. I love this shop and you are the best boss anyone could hope for."

I give her hand a squeeze. "I appreciate that."

"So… I've been doing a little research on my own."

My head snaps up from the order I'm filling out, where the math just won't add up.

I hate math. Even simple addition throws me for a loop.

"Yeah? What do you mean?" I ask.

She pulls a stack of folded papers out of her backpack. "I hope you don't think I'm meddling, but I did some research on the developer. I found something interesting."

Like what? They have billions of dollars and I don't stand a chance against them? They have mob connections, and if I don't watch my step, I'll end up at the bottom of the East River, wearing concrete shoes?

Or is it just that they, a bunch of alpha-hole masters of the universe, get everything they go after no matter what they have to destroy in the process?

So. Depressing.

"Check it out, Livvy. There are safety violations on their record. They've been cited several times." She pushes the stack in my direction, turns to a page in the middle of it, and points.

"*What?* Where did you get this?" I lean closer, but not too close, like it might bite or something.

"At the building department or whatever it's called

in City Hall. Look, it says right here what they did wrong." Jewel points to a list of issues.

Poor construction practices...

Failure to obtain permits...

Unsafe work conditions...

Could this be true? Did they really do these things?

"Holy crap. Why would a big, successful company take chances like this?" I mutter, running a finger over the words.

"I wondered that too," Jewel says, nodding. "Turns out developers are usually under tight time constraints and pressure to cut costs. I guess all of these are related to this."

Holy fucking shit. Tingles run up my spine, not because I would ever wish this kind of ill on anyone, but when it comes down to it, I kind of do. All along I've known I'm David to their Goliath, and I'll do what I have to in order to win. If I can't win, I'll at least survive.

I turn to Jewel. "This is our trump card. I can take this to Bartlett Murray and he'll have the city council block everything." My heart's pounding. Has Jewel saved the day? I like her a lot, always have, but I hardly expected this. Didn't know she had it in her.

I throw my arms around her. "Thank you so much. I never even thought to look into the developer's background. How'd you find this? Where'd you even get the idea?"

She smiles proudly. "I meditated on it, and it came to me, like a sort of message."

Now I'm sorry I asked.

She continues. What the hell, maybe she's on to something. "I've spent the last several days researching this stuff. It seems like quite the scandal. I think you can milk it, Livvy. You have to use it."

I plan to. Boy, do I plan to.

"You are a genius, Jewel. Pure genius. I'm heading straight to Bart's office. I'll read this on the way. Can you take care of things here?"

"Of course. I'm on your side. Always."

I need someone on my side.

26

LIVVY

On the subway downtown, I read everything Jewel gave me as fast as I can. Aside from the developer's actual violations, the rest of the materials are boring city and county regulations, and the penalties for not following them. Just as my eyes are about to give out from all the fine print, a picture comes into view, beautiful and clear, that this is just another greedy developer ready to cut corners when it serves their purposes. I don't mean to gloat, but Jewel is a genius, and I, at the moment, am on top of the world. The path before me, while not perfectly clear and spelled out, is at least not as blurry as it has been for the past few days, and that's a massive load off my shoulders.

Fingers crossed, things will turn around and even start going my way again.

It's funny, you don't realize how heavily some things weigh on you until they're finally shrugged off.

I go through the metal detectors at City Hall and ask someone to point me toward Bartlett's office. I could take the elevator to the third floor but instead choose the stairs. I have some nervous energy to settle and besides, want to experience the grandeur that is City Hall's fancy staircase. I approach his office, room thirty-one, but just before I do, see him walking some men out into the hallway. They are talking and laughing, and he's patting them on the back like they're old buddies.

"Don't worry, guys. I'll take care of both places. I'm on good terms with them, and I'm sure they'll listen to me."

A tall man in a dark suit says something I can't catch, but Bartlett clearly does. He drops his head back and laughs like it's the funniest thing he's ever heard, and as the men turn down the hall, one hollers back. "You're gonna love the private plane, Bart. Just wait and see."

He claps his hands together like a happy little kid, and ducks back into his office.

Are those men… who I think they are?

I think quickly.

I walk into Bart's office and stop before the receptionist's desk. "Oh, hello. I'm supposed to be in the meeting with Bart and the developers. I haven't missed it, have I?"

The receptionist looks at me with a kind smile. "You did. The meeting just broke. But I think Bart's in his office if you want to talk to him—"

I raise my hands like a *stop* sign. "No, no. Please don't bother him. Let me catch up with the guys. They're probably gonna kill me for being late, but the traffic was so bad—"

I bolt out the door and to a bench at the far end of the hallway. My heart's pounding so hard I can't hear.

Think, Livvy, think.

Did I just see what I thought I saw? Was that Bartlett sucking up to the very developers looking to ruin my life?

Has he been in their pocket all along? Is that why he's seemed so strange lately?

Fuck all. I need to listen to my instincts better.

One moment I'm on top of the world and the next, I'm put back in my place so fast I've got whiplash. It's like the universe is a cruel bully, teasing me with possibilities only to slam the door in my face when I finally think I'm making progress. I can't take these developer violations to Bartlett—if he's in bed with them, he won't do a damn thing and further, I'll be letting on that I'm preparing to fight. Might as well let him think this is a slam dunk for him and his cronies until the last possible moment.

I run down the stairs to catch up to the developers.

They're so busy patting each other on the back, they don't care who overhears them. And boy, do I listen carefully.

"Don't worry, that old blowhard is so easy to snow over. As soon as we've broken ground, we can blow him off."

"Exactly. And he's never stepping foot in our private plane. He and that wife of his are so annoying I'd have to bail out with a parachute. And I'm afraid of heights!"

The men laugh and laugh, fist bumping and slapping each other on the back. I keep my head down as they pass by me to catch a cab, but I see how on top of the world they all are. They've got nothing to worry about, that's how confident they are they'll get their way.

That's because they don't know who they're messing with. Yet.

27

LIVVY

> Emergency meeting. Now.

> Are you OK?

> Not sure. Be there in 10

I GIVE the guys a heads up that we need to meet, then hop in a cab back to the Upper East Side, something I rarely do because I'm thrifty, but time is of the essence.

While my driver races uptown, I watch New York City whip by like a movie on fast forward. When I'm too dizzy from watching, I turn back to the stack of papers in my lap. It's funny how quickly things change.

Earlier, after I'd spotted the developer guys, I was defeated and out of my mind with despair. There was nothing left to do but get back to the shop and put together my exit plan. I was done for, and so was Pawsh Pets. But on the way out, I spotted the city planning and development office. The door was wide open, so I ducked in to see what they were all about.

I might have struck gold.

Before my cab even comes to a complete stop in front of EastSide, I jump out and charge into the restaurant. Waiting, I tap my foot until Owen sees me.

"Hey, I got your text. What's up?" he asks, bending close. Damn, he smells good. "Your face is red. Are you okay?"

He's right. I'm all worked up and out of breath. "Do you have a moment? Can you grab the guys?"

His face is covered with concern. "Sure. Take a seat. I'll be right back." He gestures toward a banquette in the corner, the same one I sat in the night before.

Less than five minutes later, we're all together. The mood is different from last night though. This time we're all business. Hanky panky is the last thing on our minds.

At least mine.

Well, sort of. Weston did grab the seat next to me and now his hand is on my thigh. I consider pushing it off. I need to focus, dammit.

But I let it stay.

"Guys, I was just at City Hall."

They lean closer, and I tell them about the developer's violations that Jewel found, and the men coming out of Bartlett Murray's office.

"Holy shit," Enzo says. "That's why he was so weird about having animals in the restaurant. He's getting a kickback from the developers. He wants us out of here just as much as they do."

"If not more," Weston adds.

"I can't believe I stumbled on all this. It's just incredible," I say. "According to the planning and development office, which I stopped by before I left, there are these things called urban preservation statutes, and they protect certain kinds of buildings. I know the buildings we're in are old. We can apply to the commission. If our buildings are accepted for protection, they can't kick us out."

Owen taps his finger against his chin. "You know, guys, I think we might already have this sort of designation. If I remember correctly, it's in our lease. It keeps us from making too many changes as the leaseholders. For example, we can't cover up that brick wall over there, or remove any of those old beams along the ceiling."

Weston smacks his hand on the table. "Holy shit. You're right. I totally forgot that. I'll go dig out the lease and see what our lawyer has to say. Hell yeah," he yells, high fiving the guys.

"Hey. What about me?" I ask.

"I got something way better for you, beautiful," he

says, leaning over and placing a nice, juicy kiss right on my lips.

He pulls away and the sound of his shoes on the tile floor gets quieter as he hustles to his office. In the meantime, I'm still sitting here with my eyes closed, relishing his kiss.

This is not lost on Owen and Enzo.

"Look at our girl, all hot and bothered," Enzo chants.

"What? No, I'm not. I closed my eyes for a second. I'm… tired, for heaven's sake. I didn't sleep in my own bed last night."

Owen narrows his eyes at me. "That's true, you didn't. But you slept pretty well, from what I could tell. Remember, I was there." He reaches for my hand, and I shake him off.

"Whatever, guys," I say in protest. "Look, we have serious business to take care of here."

Enzo is amused. "I'd call what happened last night pretty damn serious." He looks at Owen. "Wouldn't you agree, buddy?"

Owen nods gravely and I have to accept my defeat. These guys will always be able to one-up me, no matter how hard I try to stay on top. I'm just not as clever—or as asshole-ish— as they are.

I give them my best stink eye.

And end up laughing.

"Anyway, thank you for digging into this, Livvy.

You're amazing," Enzo says. "I don't know what we'd do without you."

I bet they don't, especially since they were all too happy to kick me out of my own space so they could have it for themselves.

I'm not bitter, though.

Hell, maybe my business will explode at some point, and I can kick *them* out.

28

WESTON

"HEY GUYS, thanks for coming up here. I know it's tight."

That's an understatement. Restaurants rarely waste prime real estate on offices. Why would we when we can use the space for either cooking or serving food? You know, something that makes money.

But to call the space where I spend most of my days an 'office' is definitely looking on the bright side of things. There's room for a desk and a chair, a small filing cabinet, and our safe. Behind me is a tiny bookshelf piled high with papers.

Regardless, I just asked Owen, Enzo, and Livvy here to share some important info. Yes, it's cozy, but it's not going to kill anyone.

Owen slings an arm around Livvy's shoulder and she nudges him in the ribs. "Good thing we all like each other," he says.

"Who's saying I like you, Owen?" she asks, frowning. "Or any of you?"

I have to laugh at that.

He grabs her and gives her a pretend noogie. She shoulder chucks him back.

I wait until they are done horsing around. "You ready now, children?"

"Yeah, how old are you two? Twelve?" Enzo asks, his grin sly.

I know what he's thinking. He'd like to be the one messing around with Livvy right now.

She straightens up and shakes Owen off. "So this is where it all happens?" she asks, looking around. "I have to say, it's nicer than my office over at Pawsh. At least yours doesn't smell like kitty litter."

"Maybe not, but let me tell you, when they're cooking fish downstairs, the air gets really thick up here. That I hate fish makes it even worse."

Ah yes, the glamourous life of the small business owner. Some days, the grind is rough. Other days not so much.

I clap my hands together. "Our lawyer's looking over the lease to see if there's language in there that might protect us. But he also wants to run with Livvy's find, that we try to make the case that our businesses contribute to the 'cultural fabric' of the community."

Livvy laughs. "All we have to do is convince the neighborhood that a fancy restaurant and pet boutique are 'cultural.'"

"Don't give up yet. It's worked in other parts of the city. Why not here on the Upper East Side?"

The guys nod slowly while Livvy bites her lip. I know she feels vulnerable, and that sucks for her. We guys have each other, but Livvy must feel like she's hanging out there all on her own. I doubt that's a comfortable place to be.

I've grown to like her the past couple weeks, and I want to help her any way I can—almost more than I want to help EastSide. We guys have access to investors and have a track record of running a successful business. We have options. We have people who believe in us. Should EastSide fail? There's any number of other things we can do professionally.

I doubt it's the same for Livvy. Sure, she could work as a dog walker or get a job in that big box pet store across town. I shudder when I think what a blow that would be.

But I see a glimmer of hope and I really want everyone else to, as well.

"Guys, this could be great. I feel really good about this," I say.

Everyone looks at Livvy. It's funny how, in the short time we've spent with her, we all have a sense of protectiveness toward her. We don't want anything to hurt her, if we can help it.

That's the rub—we only have so much influence.

But I don't think it's an exaggeration to say we're almost more invested in making sure Pawsh Pets makes it than EastSide. Not that we don't love our restaurant, it's just that Livvy needs our help.

She needs us.

Maybe even, on some level, we need her.

"Livvy, you're going to be okay. I know it," I say.

She presses her lips together and nods, and while she's looking down, I swear her eyes are tearing.

I switch places with Enzo, no easy feat since we both have to suck it in big time to pass each other. I step on his toes and he yelps, but I am finally standing in front of our beautiful girl.

I hook a finger under her chin and turn her to face me. I was right, she's getting choked up.

"Hey," I say softly, "you all right, sweetie?"

She looks up at me with watery eyes, and sniffles. "Yeah. I… appreciate your confidence. I wish I felt the same way. Sure, we had a small victory today, but I don't feel as positive as you that things will go our way. I'm glad I've teamed up with you guys, don't get me wrong. I'd be nowhere without your clout and resources, but who's to say that if and when we beat the developers, you won't come to me again, wanting to take over my space?"

And there we have it. The elephant in the room.

The guys and I haven't discussed our expansion plans since we found out we needed to put our energy into saving what we already have. But I feel safe speaking for all of us.

"Look, Livvy. That was insensitive of us, to barge in there like we did. Talk about a dick move. And I will be the first to admit, I was driving all that. I'm sorry. I can tell you right now that any expansion plans are off the table until we resolve this. And when they come up for discussion again, your shop will not be the space we target."

"Yea. Sure," she says, looking at me through damp eyelashes.

"I'm sorry you don't have more trust in us."

She's so beautiful and vulnerable at that moment I can't help but grab her arms and pull her to me. I've been around so many sharks, so many people who think nothing of eating alive a woman like Livvy that it feels damn good to finally do something to help one of them.

She's just the sort of person my father would steam-roll, the bastard. He'd hate that I'm spending my time and energy on a 'nobody' who is going 'nowhere.'

Go to hell, Dad.

I'm not letting anything happen to her.

My lips crash into hers in a rough, hard kiss. She flings her arms around me and props her ass on the edge of my desk, opening her legs to make space for me. As she pulls me closer, her skirt rides up, and Enzo wastes no time waiting to run his fingers over her soft thighs.

She sigh-moans into my mouth, and I know this moment is a release for us both. The pressure and uncertainty of our futures dangles in the balance, no one's more so than hers, and it's time to blow off some of that steam.

"Look at Wes," Owen sings when I reach for the thin strip of fabric covering Livvy's pussy.

I rub her up and down there, right on the spot where she's hot and damp, and damn if she doesn't scoot closer, begging for more like the hungry little bird she is.

I'd love to fuck this woman right here, right now on my desk, but this isn't how I want our first time to be. Yes, I say first time, because I expect there will be a second, third, and more. If she's down with that, of course.

But that doesn't mean we can't have some other adult fun in my little office today.

I nod at Enzo, who clears my desk of its keyboard and stacks of papers, and lean Livvy back. I prop her feet next to her hips on the desk, opening her wide, and while there is still a layer of silky fabric between us, I can smell her excitement. It about sends me over my edge.

I want nothing more than to take my cock out and jerk it all over her pretty panties. But first things first.

Enzo bends to kiss her, and I push aside the fabric covering her pussy. What I find is glistening and pink and ready. So ready.

For me.

I part her lips slightly and flick her with my tongue. She shudders, and I do it again. Then, I run a finger around her clit, down to her sex, and slide it inside her pussy, warm and easily slipping in and out of its wetness. I run the same finger down to her ass and tickle her there for a moment, just to see what she does.

She likes it.

I return my tongue to her pussy, running up and down and slurping everything between her lips like a man dying of dehydration. I want to consume every bit of what she gives me, that's how badly I want her.

I slip a second finger inside her, and zero in on her clit with my tongue. In seconds she's bucking her hips against my face.

"Oh god yes," she cries.

Her heat intensifies and she tightens around my fingers, pulsing and squeezing as she begins to come.

"Fuck yeah," one of the guys mumbles.

I don't know which one. It doesn't matter. My thoughts are filled with the vibrations of this woman beneath me, shaking and crying and grasping the heady luxury and power of sensual pleasure, just the way she deserves it.

She's still shaking when she opens her eyes and looks at me. "More," she whispers. "I want more."

Well, damn.

I turn her so she's bent over the side of the desk. I

lift her skirt all the way to her hips, and then slide her panties down so they're hanging on one ankle. Pushing her feet apart with my own, I open my trousers and in seconds, I'm poised at her opening.

So much for waiting for the perfect first time.

"You ready, baby?" I ask, leaning next to her ear.

Face down on the desk, she nods. "Yes. Please. Give it to me."

I tease my hard-on up and down her wet slit. "Give you what, Livvy? What do you want me to give you?"

"Don't be a jerk, Wes," she whines.

"I wanna hear it, baby."

She slaps her hand on the desk in frustration. "I want your cock, Wes," she breathes. "I want you to fuck me."

Goddamn, I love a dirty girl, especially one who's right next door.

I push inside her just an inch and she gasps. "Like this, baby? Is this how you want my cock?"

She giggles. "Dammit, Wes, quit messing with me."

Okay then. I drive my cock all the way inside her, so hard her feet lift off the floor, and she has to hold onto the desk to keep from flying off.

"Oh God," she screams, followed by some of the sexiest moans I've ever heard.

I drive in and out of her pussy, every inch of my body pulsing with need, and when I erupt inside her, my senses shut down. All I can feel is her milking every drop of cum out of me.

29

WESTON

THE RESTAURANT BUSINESS waits for no one.

I won't lie, I was up half the night replaying Livvy's sweet orgasm on my office desk, to the point where I jerked myself sore and still couldn't get to sleep.

So, in spite of the fact that I'm hoping for a slow day, the moment I arrive at work, the restaurant is already chaos-central. Nothing life-threatening, but the staff would have me think otherwise.

One of the kitchen crew, a new girl with purple hair and a tattoo around her neck, bursts into my office where I'm still straightening things up from playtime the night before.

"Wes, there's been a supplier mixup," she says breathlessly.

"Okay. What's up?"

"Well," she begins, wringing her hands and on the edge of tears, "instead of olive oil, they sent us *truffle oil.*"

She says it like they sent us a bag of horse shit or something, that's how disturbed she is. I don't bother reminding her that we actually use truffle oil in our heirloom tomato dish, among other things. The woman is clearly partial to olive oil.

I grab my iPad to look up our recent orders. "Okay, hang on. Let me see what's up."

As I scroll, she gets increasingly worked up. "Also, Wes, I can't find the balsamic. I think we're all out. I need it for the vegetable reduction."

"What does Enzo say?"

"He told me to tell you."

Thanks, buddy.

I'm having trouble making sense of the orders in front of me, so I reach into my pocket and pull out a couple twenties. "Here you go. Run to the corner store and get what you need for now. I'll straighten this out with the supplier."

She holds her chin up bravely. "Good thinking, Wes. I'll take care of that right now."

With a nod, she leaves my office, her sneakered feet clomping all the way down the stairs until I can't hear her anymore.

Jesus. Did I mess up an order? Or two? I never do shit like this. No doubt I've been distracted lately, what with the developer issues and all, not to mention how getting to 'know' Livvy has taken up space in my brain. And yet, I still don't understand how I could be messing things up. I'm the 'numbers guy.' I'm logical, uptight, anal—you name it—and that's what makes me good at what I do. My lack of emotion drives Owen and Enzo crazy sometimes, but they don't seem to complain when I show them how profitable our little venture has become.

I wonder if they're as distracted as I am?

Just then, Owen pops his head in. "Dude," he says, his expression a mix of amusement and wanting to murder someone. "I just got a complaint that someone's bruschetta is too crispy."

Jesus fucking Christ.

Over-crispy bruschetta. Funny-not-funny.

"Is it who I think it is?" I ask.

Every restaurant has its share of notoriously difficult regulars and EastSide is no exception. For the most part, regulars are a blessing. But there will always be a few who believe that since they come by all the time and drop a shitload of dough, they are entitled to a level of VIP service that's all but impossible to provide.

"Yeah. You know, the older woman with the big round glasses. She's a hoot, but she loves nothing more than tearing me a new asshole in front of her old-lady friends. It's like she comes here just for that purpose, to show how much clout she has."

I've no doubt Owen would like to tell this woman to go fuck herself, but you can't do that, not in the restaurant business, nor in any business, no matter how abusive the customers get. Jesus, that would be rich, for the entire Upper East Side to find out that one of the owners yelled at a sweet old lady who made a simple little request. News like that travels faster than a New York minute. Our business would dry up so goddamn fast it wouldn't matter that there are developers after our space.

Restaurant life is crazy, but I love it. Stupid shit like this morning's, minor annoyances in the grand scheme of things, remind me of what I get out of bed in the morning for.

After Owen lets off his steam, I head down to the basement to check the wine cellar inventory. I'm entering the cool, dark room to make sure I haven't screwed up those orders when my phone lights up. I consider ignoring it because when it comes to our wines, I really can't mess up—we make too much money from them—but when I see it's our lawyer, I jump on the call. Nothing else could get my heart pounding right now than hearing from him.

"Wes, I've got news," he says.

I brace myself for impact. Our attorney is a real poker face and you never know if what's coming at you is going to be good or bad.

"Fill me in," I say.

"I think we can get a temporary injunction based on the info you provided."

"Hell yeah!" I scream, my voice echoing back from the dark corners of the cellar.

I doubt anyone up in the restaurant heard me, but I also don't care if they did. I'll take this bit of good news. I need it, dammit. We all do. I finally feel like we're on the offensive rather than continually playing defense. It might be a small win, but I'll take the motherfucker.

A victory, no matter how small, calls for celebration. So between lunch and dinner service, I run over to Pawsh Pets to make sure Livvy leaves her evening open for us guys.

"Hello, Weston," her assistant Jewel says in a flat, droning voice.

"Jewel. Nice to see you."

Silence.

"Yeah, well, is Livvy here?" I ask, wondering why she's looking at me like she wants to kill me.

More silence.

Then, she screams at the top of her lungs. "Livvy!"

Her banshee-like wail startles the shit out of me, that's how unexpected it was. Cripes, how does Livvy work with her?

"What is it, Jewel?" Livvy asks as she runs from the back of the store. She's soaked, almost from head to toe, and is wiping her hands on her smock.

"Wes, hi," she says, a shy smile growing across her face.

There's my beautiful girl.

Shit. Did I say that out loud?

"Livvy, we got good news from our attorney. Come by later tonight and we'll celebrate."

She clasps her hands together and jumps up and down in her rubber boots. "No way, that's incredible. Is he getting the temporary injunction?"

"It looks like it. Keep in mind it's not a done deal, but we'll take whatever victory we can get, right?"

She closes her fists and squeezes her eyes, and shimmies like she won the damn lottery or something. "I don't care. It's a step in the right direction."

From the back of the shop, I hear a dog whining.

"Oh crap. I'm grooming someone's pup. Gotta go," she says, and runs to the back of the store, leaving wet footprints behind her.

I turn back to Jewel. I feel like I need to say something to her but I come up empty.

"She's gonna be a while," she says, nodding toward the back of the shop. "She's gotta do the anal glands yet."

I'm pretty sure that's my signal to go.

30

WESTON

I WAS PLANNING for a low-key after-hours celebration for Livvy, the guys, and me, but to be honest, we just don't do low-key. Top-shelf liquor and gourmet vegetarian hors d'oeuvres are how we roll. And when Livvy walks in, her dog grooming duds long gone, she looks damn good in a swingy little red dress and high heels. It's not that she isn't attractive all the time, but tonight, seeing her all cleaned up after a dirty day in the shop, she's positively glowing, like she showered in something special, something that promises the ethereal glow I see before me right now.

She walks into EastSide, and the guys greet her warmly, taking turns kissing her and taking her by the hand to the kitchen, which she's never seen. She waves to me where I stand on the other side of the room, and I watch her face light up under the attention of the guys.

I'll admit my feelings for this woman are more than just physical, even if that's how they started. I respect her. She's scrappy as hell, always ready to put up a fight for what she believes in.

When the rest of the restaurant staff is gone, we open a bottle of champagne and hold our glasses up for a toast right there in the freshly-cleaned kitchen.

"To Livvy. We would have made no progress if not for you," Owen says.

She does an exaggerated curtsey. "Yeah, I'm just the rainmaker here, aren't I?"

Enzo shrugs one shoulder. "Don't sell yourself short, beautiful. We wouldn't be where we are without your work."

"I have to say, Jewel gets the credit. She's the one who got the ball rolling with the developer's violations. Ya know?"

"Cheers to Jewel. We owe her a bottle of champagne, for sure," I say.

I hope I'm not the one who has to deliver it to her. Just saying.

We gather our kitchen stools around one of the stainless-steel prep tables, and sample the goodies Enzo's team made us, including truffled custard in egg shells, cheese puffs with black garlic and fennel pollen, and compressed watermelon and tomato terrine.

"I guess you guys never eat normal appetizers, like pigs in a blanket? Chips 'n dip?" Livvy asks.

She got us. Everything we do is to the Nth degree of fanciness. What can I say?

"Hold on," Owen says, jumping to his feet. He runs off to the big refrigerator walk-in.

"Where's he going?" Livvy asks.

Enzo shakes his head. "He keeps a stash of his own crap hidden away. Let's see what he brings back."

"Here we go," Owen says, reaching into a grocery bag with 'sweetbreads' written across the front of it.

"Sweetbreads?" Livvy gags. "That's not really what I was thinking when I brought up 'normal food.'"

"Ha. That's just my decoy. Keeps nosy people out of my snacks."

He reaches in and pulls out two cans of Pringles chips.

Good work, buddy. I fucking love Pringles.

"Give me those," Livvy says, lunging at Owen.

But he holds them out of her reach.

She raises her hands in surrender. "Fine. Whatever, I can go buy my own damn chips. In fact, I think I'll go do that right now."

She starts down from her stool, but Enzo swings an arm around her waist to catch her. He deftly pulls her onto his lap and in spite of her wriggling, won't let her get away. Her champagne sloshes all over the two of them, and she's laughing her ass off.

"I want chips, dammit," she hollers.

This is what I like to see. A woman who can laugh at herself—hell, who can laugh at all the crazy things going on around her. Who doesn't take herself too seriously. Who understands that life at its best is usually an absurd shitshow, and who doesn't let it get her down.

After she settles, Enzo helps himself to the soft skin on the side of her neck. Her eyes flutter closed and he brushes his lips over her, and Owen takes her champagne glass before it smashes to the floor.

The weighty question of 'what are we?' hangs in the air as if we're all wondering it but not sure we should say it out loud. But it's obvious as fuck, and even though I haven't discussed it with the guys, I decide to speak for all of us.

"Baby," I say, and her eyes slowly open. She focuses on me, and the guys turn my way as well.

They know what's coming. So does she.

"What do you think about... you know... dating us?"

She tilts her head. "Like all three of you?"

I nod, and Enzo pipes in. "It's complicated, darlin'. But we'd like to give it a go."

"Wow. Geez," she says.

Shit. Is she stalling for time? Trying to think of a nice way to let us down?

"It's sure not traditional," she muses. "But then not much about me is," she laughs, pulling Owen to her for a kiss.

A wild, reckless hope plows over me and for a moment I think everything will be fine. Fine with the restaurant, the pet shop next door, and with Livvy. The Earth will keep rotating, the sun will keep coming up every morning, and I'll keep serving fancy food to people on the Upper East Side of New York.

That's all I want, really.

31

LIVVY

I ARRIVE at Krista and Carter's house—*Kritterdom*, I call it, since they are the Kritters—but before I go inside, I consider the grandeur of the life my sister managed to marry into when she sunk her hooks into my now-brother-in-law.

I take in her McMansion from the curved drive out front. It's the kind of house you find on those snarky websites that make fun of ostentatious suburban homes. It's quite something, the Kritters's house, with its turret, giant French doors, and perfectly coiffed landscaping.

Personally, I prefer my dinky apartment in the city.

It was never a secret that Krista liked the finer things in life and if anything, her ambitions were supported by my mother, who never made it out of what she saw as the drudgery of the middle class. Mom made sure Krista went to the best summer camps, had the prettiest clothes of any girl in her class, the most lavish birthday parties—even if it meant she had to take extra shifts at the furniture store where she worked to afford it.

As for me, they never understood why I wasn't interested in any of that crap, only tagging along when I had to. I was the weirdo. The odd man out. Still am.

When Krista got her hooks into Carter, she was somehow able to overlook his creepiness, and she never let him go. He was her ticket out of the 'burbs we grew up in, and she wasn't missing that train, no matter what. She went as far as to try and convince him she was a virgin when they met and that their wedding night would be her first time doing the deed.

I'll never know how she got away with that. I'll also never be the one to tell him his chaste wife is full of shit and was a big old ho at summer camp.

What he doesn't know won't hurt him.

I take a deep breath before I ring the doorbell, knowing some smiling servant-for-hire will be letting me in, looking over my shoulder for a companion.

I hate to break it to you, Jeeves, but there's no date for old Livvy tonight.

My plan was to take Arthur as my plus-one, but he bailed thanks to one of his flight attendant friends coming to town.

I considered bringing Jewel but ruled that out pretty quickly. I adore her, I do, but one never knows when she's going to practice her method acting, or spring one of her crystal readings on someone.

I know I could have invited one of the guys from EastSide, but how the hell could I choose? I am still getting to know them and am a long way from being able to make any sort of decision. If it even comes to that.

Which, I am sure, it won't.

The amazing thing is that none of them has gotten on my nerves yet, which is a total freaking miracle, not to mention as unlikely as hell freezing over.

Take Owen. My bad, I originally thought he was a stick-up-his-ass hipster. He's actually a decent, charming guy just trying to make it in the world, who's in the closet about owning a pet cat.

Weston is much quieter and in fact doesn't really talk much about himself, but I can tell he comes from a privileged background. I have to hand it to him for all the hard work he does for EastSide, when he probably really doesn't have to.

And Enzo, sweet, sweet Enzo, who looks after his nonna with a dedication the rest of us could only ever hope for. I know he's behind the insane vegetarian dishes the guys have been plying me with, even though he never takes credit for any of it.

They're good guys when it comes down to it, not to mention gorgeous, sexy, attentive…

Why am I here at my sister's tonight?

The door person at the Kritters lets me in and takes my trench coat, a hand-me-down from my sister. I'm not sure whether I should just walk into the room where I can see people mingling and having pre-dinner drinks, or if I have to be escorted by the hired help. So, while I wait for my coat to be put wherever they put things like that, I look around the massive foyer, which has more crystal chandeliers than a royal palace. Not that I've ever been in a royal palace.

I'm immediately hit with the aromas of a multi-course meal, complete with waitstaff and a sommelier for an extra touch, none of whom give a shit that I'm a vegetarian. In fact, I'll bet my entire store that I'm presented with a plate full of some kind of charred animal flesh. If I say anything, the Kritters will snap and tell me to just eat my veggies.

And to shut up.

Well, they won't say that part. It will be understood by everyone in hearing distance.

It turns out I am the last to arrive, so as soon as Krista spots me, she corrals everyone to the dining table, denying me the opportunity to suck down a cocktail hour martini or two that would help dull the pain of the evening. I knew I should have left the city earlier.

Everyone takes their seat at the long dining room table according to the name plates Krista set out, so it's no accident I'm seated between two guys who I can safely assume are single and looking. The one on my left giggles every time he looks my way, and the one on my other side wheezes when he breathes.

Thanks, Krista and Carter, for the top shelf choices you always provide me.

After Carter toasts Krista as if she made the whole meal herself, he goes around the table introducing each of the guests and how he came to know them. My stomach growls loudly, but when I reach for the dinner roll on my bread plate, Krista gives me a dirty look. I smile back and snatch it to my lap when she looks away, breaking off tiny pieces and shoveling them in my mouth, letting them dissolve on my tongue rather than risk being caught chewing.

None too soon, dinner is served and just like I knew would happen, I am facing down some kind of lamb dish. I push my vegetables away so they're not touching the meat and look around the table for another poor soul in my same position. If there's another vegetarian present, they are doing a good job of hiding it.

Halfway through the evening, Krista turns to me from her end of the table, and I brace myself for whatever inappropriate thing she's about to announce.

"Say, Olive, still enjoying the single life in Manhattan?" she calls down the length of the table.

"Livvy," I say to everyone gathered. "The name is Livvy."

They nod politely.

How my love life could be interesting enough to

discuss in front of a bunch of strangers is beyond me, but she's done such a great job getting everyone's attention that there are now twenty pairs of eyes staring at me, waiting for my response.

Her voice oozes with false concern, but I know how to fight fire with fire. I've had a lot of practice.

I smile pleasantly to cut through any sisterly tension. "Absolutely, Krista, having a great time. After all, I'm not bored or desperate enough yet to settle."

I pick up my fork and stab the last green bean on my plate. "Mmmm," I murmur, "these are so good."

Polite titters flow around the table and I wish there were a scoreboard so I could give myself one point, and my sister, a big fat zero.

The evening progresses and the wheezer and giggler aren't so bad if you keep your expectations low enough. They each ask for my number when the other isn't listening, and I assure them that I'll share 'my digits' after dinner to keep things discreet.

Yes, I'm lying. So what?

Just as I start to think I may be leaving the Kritters dinner party wearing no further wounds from insults hurled my way, I realize there's no such luck. Because, why would there be? My brother-in-law Carter, who wears his douchey-ness like a teenage boy wears Axe Body Spray, dive bombs me.

"How's the boutique pet business, Livvy? Selling the hell out of those artisanal hamster wheels?"

He chuckles with a practiced *har-har-har*, and in

spite of myself and all the things going my way, a part of me crumbles. I know I shouldn't let him get to me, but in a room of tech moguls and venture capitalists, I stand out like a sore thumb. I have no place here. My sister invites me as a show of some sort of humanity, like trotting out a rescue dog to show the world you have a soft side.

My previous jauntiness is now pretty much deflated and the chocolate mousse dessert before me just looks disgusting.

I've always been the odd one out. I'm used to that.

It's the same with the EastSide guys and me. I have no place messing around with them. As soon as this developer drama is put to rest, they'll be back to their Manhattan glamazons, and I'll be expressing canine anal glands next door in my Birkenstocks and dirty smock.

32

LIVVY

I STARE out the window of my Uber all the way home. Carter insisted he call me one on his account to show off his largesse. Typical, *look how I take care of my little sister-in-law* crap. Had it been just the two of us, he would have said good luck getting home and shut the door in my face.

But hey, I'm not too proud to save fifty dollars to get home, especially not after a night like tonight.

Why did I think this evening might be different? Every time I go to the Kritters, it ends the same way. I swear I'll never go back and yet I always do.

What is wrong with me?

The second I'm home I kick my shoes off and open the *New York Times* crossword on my phone. I can really only manage the easy puzzles days, Mondays and Tuesdays, so I go back through the archive to look for an old one that won't make me feel like a total dunce.

That's when my phone pings with an email notification, a proposal from the developer. I scroll through the legalese and find the fuckers answered every 'loophole' as they call them, that the guys and I found.

Historic building? Nope.

Culturally important? Nope.

Safety violations? Disappeared.

What in the fucking fuck?

It's too much. Just too much. A shitty night at my sister's and then news like this? In what world does the universe just keep dumping on someone who's already down on their luck?

Sucks. Just fucking sucks.

I'm way too annoyed now to continue with my crossword and when I pull out BOB from my nightstand, I twist it on for a little solo action. But don't you know before the thing is even freaking warmed up, the battery dies.

I must have really fucked someone over in a past life. That's all I can figure. Someone or something is getting even with me and laughing their ass off while doing it.

I go to my laptop and pull up the developer's proposal so I can see it full-size and my stomach sinks further with every page I read. Crafty bastards. I can see their wrecking ball right now, all wrapped in a pretty bow, demolishing Pawsh Pets and along with it every dream I've ever had.

But the truth is, *I* might manage to singlehandedly demolish Pawsh Pets before the developers even arrive. The stack of unpaid and overdue bills in my desk drawer is growing deeper, and I can't avoid the inevitable for much longer.

I am sure Owen, Weston, and Enzo got the same email from the developer and are probably looking at it with the same contempt I am. How we can continue to fight these people without looking insanely unreasonable is beyond me. I let my fingers hover over the keyboard, unsure of what to type before I close it down for the night. I don't need any more trouble and threatening these people with bodily harm will do no one any good, least of all me.

Next morning, I force myself to focus on Pawsh business rather than running over to EastSide to bitch about the latest developer development. I don't need the guys next door to think I'm any more neurotic than I already am.

It doesn't take long for *them* to show up at *my* door.

Something about that feels good.

"We gotta talk," Owen says.

"Guys, let's go to the coffee shop down the street," I say. "Jewel, will you hold down the fort?"

"Yes, Livvy," she says, glaring at the guys.

I don't know why she doesn't like them.

"Can I get you anything?" Owen asks me when we arrive.

Yes, I want to say. But there are so many things I need right now, I wouldn't know where to start.

"No thanks," I say, my shoulders slumping.

Enzo throws a casual arm around me. "Oh, Livvy, don't worry. We'll get this all sorted."

Maybe he's right. Maybe we'll get the business with the developers sorted.

What he doesn't know is that's not the end of my problems. In fact, it's not even my biggest. No one knows Pawsh Pets is struggling financially. No one besides me and my creditors.

I consider my options for the hundredth time.

I could move out in the middle of the night like the shoe store across the street did. Leave New York, provide no forwarding address. Just disappear into the night.

I could let the guys buy me out like they offered weeks ago. Negotiate from their initial offer so I get a bit more payout and live off the proceeds while I figure out what to do next.

Or I could walk into a busy street and get hit by a cab.

Actually, scratch that. I've heard being hit by a car can be painful if you are not instantly killed.

Owen returns with three coffees for himself and the guys, and a heart-shaped sugar cookie for me.

"Awww," I say. "A sweet treat." I unwrap it and take

a huge bite, offering to share it with no one. I need this cookie. Badly.

Weston puts his hands on the table. "Okay, everybody. I know this is not something any of you want to hear, but I think the developer's offer is... not really that bad."

I choke on a crumb and wish I'd let Owen bring me something to drink. I cough hard, patting my chest and dabbing my watering eyes, but no one notices.

They're looking at Weston and he's looking back at them. I could be bleeding out and I doubt they'd notice at this particular moment.

It's good to know where I stand.

No one says anything for a moment, and then everyone talks at once.

"Are you fucking kidding..."

"No way. No way we're taking a buyout..."

"So... we just roll over and play dead...."

"Dude, have you lost your goddamn mind..."

"It's just one setback. We can't throw in the towel yet..."

Weston lets the three of us throw a multitude of objections his way, both polite and indignant. His pleasant expression never falters, as if he has an invisible shield protecting him. It's only when the bitching dies down that he starts talking again, like the whole conversation is choreographed.

But no one's really listening, I can tell. I know I'm not, lost in thought as I am. It's like someone put cotton in my ears and I can hear blah-blah-blah, and that's it. I watch Enzo's gaze dart back and forth between Weston and Owen like he's waiting for one of them to take the first swing. Business partnerships have broken up over less.

I'm torn. Torn between logic and stubborn pride, between new possibilities and suffocating doubt. There are no easy answers, as evidenced not only by the rising voices at our table, but also my own silent retreat from the conversation and the matter as a whole.

If I shrink away quietly enough, I can hide, and none of this bullshit can reach me.

Right?

33

ENZO

BEFORE WE BREAK up our meeting at the coffee shop—the one that went from bad to worse with every passing minute—we invite Livvy for dinner. She waffles, so I offer to do it at my house. Maybe she's getting sick of EastSide.

But she ultimately shoots us down. No big surprise. Poor thing is so dejected I don't know how she got out of bed this morning. We walk back to our block, dropping her at Pawsh Pets. I give her the biggest, juiciest hug I can muster and wonder if she can hear the heart thumping in my chest.

Yes, I'm a sensitive guy. I'll admit it.

"Hey," I say, hooking a finger under her chin until

she's looking at me, "if you need anything, and I mean anything, you know how to reach me."

She responds with a wan smile, the kind someone with the flu gives you when they want you to think they don't really feel that badly.

"Look. I'll come over with a snack later, okay?"

She nods and we guys get back to work.

The rest of the day I just go through the motions, overseeing the cooks and all the dishes they put together, but my heart's not really in it. Instead, I have vegetarian ingredients running through my thoughts, creating all sorts of combinations—ones that will appeal to Livvy, of course. I scribble down a recipe and pass it to my best cook, telling him it's an experiment I want to try.

A couple hours later, when things quiet down, I sneak out of the restaurant with my new creation in hand, violet aspic with goat cheese mousse.

In my chef whites, I run to Pawsh Pets before anyone can see me. It's not that I'm sneaking, per se, I just don't want a shitload of questions raining down on my head from the guys, our patrons, or anyone in the neighborhood who might see me walking down the street. I don't want to be away from the restaurant for long and can't afford to shoot the shit with anyone.

Anyone other than Livvy, that is.

I duck inside the shop just as someone with three little rat dogs is coming out, laden with two large shopping bags.

Way to go, Pawsh Pets.

"Hey, Livvy."

She looks up from her computer and something in her face changes. I can't say exactly what, but it borders on some kind of happiness, which in turn makes me happy.

"Enzo, how's it going?"

I place my box with the aspic and goat cheese on the counter and retrieve a little fork and napkin from my pocket. "I made you something special. I think you'll really like it."

Her face brightens and she claps her hands together like a little girl. "You made something for *me?*"

"Oh, well, you know, I had an idea for a vegetarian dish for the restaurant and thought I'd test it out. I had one of the cooks put it together. I sampled it, of course, but I had to have a real veg give it a test."

She looks at me slyly. I don't blame her. She's no dummy and it isn't hard to figure out I don't spend my days making up weird-ass vegetarian dishes for a restaurant that uses so much meat.

I don't mind. In fact, I *want* her to know my ulterior motives.

She carefully opens the box and gasps. "Wow. This is too pretty to eat. It looks like some sort of sculpture in the front window at Tiffany. Not something meant to be consumed."

She laughs when I pass her a fork. "Just because it's too pretty to eat, doesn't mean I won't." She scoops a big bite into her mouth, closes her eyes, and moans.

Fuck yeah.

She eats the way she lives—taking big bites out of life with no worry for what others might think.

"So, you like it?" I ask as she looks into the empty box to make sure she left nothing behind.

"That, Enzo, was one of the tastiest things I've eaten in my whole life. I don't even know what it was, but it was pure heaven."

She closes her eyes and rubs her belly and all I can think is that she's the cutest fucking thing.

I take a step around the counter to get closer, and I wonder if she can feel the thick air between us, or if it's all in my imagination. Only one way to find out.

"Livvy, I've wanted to tell you… well, that I… have a lot of admiration for you. Your tenacity, sense of humor, kindness, love of animals. I gotta tell you, you fascinate me. I don't think I've ever met a woman like you."

I don't mention how she tries to hide all this under a spiky, smart-ass exterior, because, when it comes down to it, her prickly shell is about as transparent as the glass in her front window. She's not fooling anyone, least of all me.

She looks at me, her eyes wide, like she's trying to decide what to do with this information. I get that she might be ambivalent. I just laid a big load on her and hell, we don't know each other that well even if we have messed around.

As the seconds pass in silence, I find myself regretting being so frank. I should have just kept my damn thoughts to myself. My nonna always says I wear my heart on my sleeve and that's not a good look for a man. I try to tell her my generation is different but she doesn't get it.

Does she have a point?

I inch back from Livvy, thinking it's high time to split, when she busts out into a huge grin, one of those rare, full smiles that transforms a person's face.

In return, my spirits soar.

Sorry, Nonna.

She looks down at the counter, drumming her fingers on it. "This… complicates things, doesn't it?"

I don't give a fuck, I want to tell her. Life is complicated. So what?

Damn if I don't feel like I won the lottery, which is weird because it's not like I freaking asked her to marry me. I don't get it, not at all.

"Hey, you're invited to my family dinner tomorrow night. You free?" I ask.

She pretends to hold open a notebook and page through it. She's a good pantomime, and I love that she's teasing me. "I think I can squeeze you in," she laughs.

I clap my hands together. "Excellent. I gotta get back to the resto before someone burns it down."

"What can I bring?" she asks.

I look at her. "I can't think of a single thing."

34

ENZO

DINNER at my family home is not for the faint of heart, not on the best day of the year, and my bringing a guest does not guarantee a damn thing. We could laugh our asses off… or a fight could break out. We could tell stories and laugh until we cry, or argue and shout and smash dishes against the wall. There are no pretenses with my family, no 'being on our best behavior.' What you see is what you get and it's all subject to change with no advance notice.

And Livvy is the perfect person to handle something like that.

"So, Livvy, things at my family home can get a little… lively," I say, steering the borrowed car onto my parents' street. We have to park at the end of the block, that's how many cars are here. Guess no one wants to miss out on Enzo bringing a girl home.

Cripes, I should have my head examined for walking into this minefield.

Livvy scoffs as she gathers the bouquet of flowers she got for my mother. "I can handle family stuff. Don't you worry about me."

Famous last words.

As we get closer to my parents' front stoop, the cacophony that is the Messina family reaches out to the street, not limited to the smell of my mother's famous sauce, someone smoking a cigar, and shouts coming from the basement where my uncles are most likely speeding through a game of pre-dinner darts.

We greet Nonna first because, in my family, that's how it's done.

"Livvy, honey, hello. Come here and kiss me, honey," Nonna rasps from her spot on the sofa, taking Livvy's hand and pulling her down to her level with a freakish amount of strength.

"Oh my," Livvy says, throwing in a casual laugh to show she's cool with being manhandled by old grandmas.

Nonna points a crooked finger up at her. "Didn't expect me to be that strong, did you, honey? No one ever does. It's my superpower. Back in the day, I could kick anyone's ass—"

"Nonna," I interrupt, "Livvy's got to meet a lot of people. We'll come back around."

Nonna waves us away like we were just an annoyance anyway.

After getting her face patted by my mother, and her ass stared at by one of my cousins—whom I had to threaten with bodily harm—we eventually make it to the dining table after my mother screams for everyone several times. Pops emerges from the basement with various uncles and other male family members, and before he sits, he beams, shaking Livvy's hand in both of his.

You can say a lot about my family, that they're crazy, emotional, and unpredictable, but you could never say you feel any less than completely welcome at one of our gatherings.

Case in point. Mama, after she rustles up some help bringing dinner from the kitchen to the dining room, serves Livvy first.

"What the hell is that?" Nonna asks from the other end of the table.

But Livvy knows exactly what she's been served. And she can't hide her eyes filling with tears.

"You... you shouldn't have, Mrs. Messina. This must have been so much work for you."

Mama beams and acts like it's nothing that she made a vegetarian dish, a single-serving eggplant casserole just for Livvy. But I know she's pleased her hard work is appreciated.

"It was nothing, sweetheart," Mama says modestly.

I catch Pops's gaze and he nods, looks at Livvy, then looks back at me with a discreet thumbs-up.

All without Livvy seeing.

I nod back and our private conversation ends. He likes Livvy and wants me to know.

I am not as discreet as Pops and am beaming so broadly he rolls his eyes.

Yeah, it's been a long time since I brought a woman over. The majority of my waking hours are spent at the restaurant, and I don't meet many women there who fit into this part of my life. That doesn't mean I don't date them and fuck them, given the chance. It's just that there are limits to what I share. But I knew from the first time I saw Livvy making the rounds at our investor party giving out her business information that she had balls of steel and could hang in most any situation.

Including with my crazy family.

Livvy is lucky enough—or not, depending on whom you ask—to be sitting right next to Nonna at tonight's dinner. That means her attention will pretty much be monopolized by a feisty octogenarian the entire meal. While those two are nearly head-to-head, discussing something vitally important—at least to Nonna—the rest of the table chimes in with their usual banter, touching on everything from local politics, to neighborhood gossip, and the various digestive ailments of the elders at the table.

It's a total freakshow, but it's my freakshow, and I'm stoked about sharing it with Livvy.

The evening progresses without a hiccup, but I know not to tempt fate. My family is a lot, and before Livvy gets the urge to run away screaming, I ask Mama to give us some dessert to go, the excuse being that we both have early mornings.

It takes another thirty minutes to get out the door because everyone wants a hug and a kiss and a promise from Livvy that she'll come back soon. I'm glad everyone else made her promise that she would. It saved me from risking embarrassment.

On the ride back to the city, Livvy can't stop talking about the evening. She's clearly both enchanted and terrified, which is par for the course with my family.

"Your nonna is really something."

"She is. You know, when I flunked out of college, she was the only one who stood by my side. I'll never forget that."

"Seems like things have been smoothed over. Everyone loves you," she says.

"Yeah. It was a long time ago. At least it feels that way."

I surprise myself by sharing such a personal story, but I think I'm filling the silence because I don't have the balls to say what I'd really like to.

The one thing I want to ask Livvy is something I can't bring myself to—how she feels about me. It's entirely too risky for a bunch of reasons, not least of which that both our futures are on somewhat shaky ground, and who knows if we'll even all be in the city a month from now?

35

ENZO

NEXT DAY, reality smacks me right in the mouth, starting with my sous-chef calling in sick, which means I have to do his job, not that I don't want to, but I have other shit to take care of. On top of that, Owen is on the warpath because two of his waitstaff are late, and he can't cover for them. And I'm ninety-nine percent sure we received the wrong order of organic herbs, which might sound minor, but for a restaurant like EastSide that prides itself on unique dishes, nothing creates a signature like unexpected flavors. As I clean up and prepare for my shift replacing my missing sous chef, there's nothing I can do about the herbs until Weston comes in because he has all the orders on his iPad or the cloud or something like that. Sure, I could check on the office computer, but my brain does not work like his, and what is logical to him and most other people is entirely lost on me.

That's why I stick to the cooking.

The chaos of the restaurant business can either invigorate you or put you in an early grave. Being an optimist, I remind myself this crap is all part of the game, and this is what it takes to shine in the restaurant-laden world of New York City. Why let it get me down?

But on a day like today that tries even my nearly unlimited patience, there's a happy buzz in the far reaches of my thoughts that keeps reminding me it's there.

Also known as the girl next door.

Literally.

After we escaped my family's clutches the night before, I drove Livvy home and let's just say the night got even better.

While scrubbing stuff in the kitchen would make most chefs like me pissed off, the monotony of it is giving my thoughts time to wander.

To a place I wish I were right now.

It starts with dropping Livvy at her door. I knew the gods were smiling down on me when I found a parking spot right in front of her building.

"Thanks for coming to the house of Messina. You handled it like a champ," I tell her. "For the uninitiated, we're not an easy bunch."

She drops her head back on the seat and smiles dreamily. "It was such a treat." She turns to look at me. "I cannot believe your mother cooked vegetarian for me. Not even my own sister will do that. They were all so real, Enzo. So normal. And I mean that in the best way."

I know exactly what she means, and that fact that she *gets it* means she gets *me*, and I am so here for that. I lean across the console between us and run my thumb over her smooth thigh, where her dress has ridden up almost to her panties.

For fuck's sake, I've been looking at that all night, clenching my fingers into fists to keep them to myself, even under the tablecloth, where no one would have known except us. But I behaved like a good boy.

She shivers lightly at my touch and even though the interior of the car is dim, I can see enough of her in the ambient streetlights to know she's giving me a sly look.

I knew she had it in her.

"What are you doing?" she asks in a sing-song voice.

I shift in my seat because, of course, my blue jeans are getting awfully tight in the dick area, and I twist a hank of her hair around my free hand. The way she smells is mind-blowing, it always is, but in the confines of the car, even though it's subtle—just inviting and fresh and clean—it's like a freaking contact high.

"I was wondering, Livvy, what kind of panties you're wearing under that pretty dress."

Even in the dark, I can see her eyes widen and her

lips open. And when I move my fingers further up her thigh, nearly to her panties, I brush her tender skin and I'll be goddamned if her legs don't part the smallest bit.

Fuck me. If she keeps this shit up, I might have to propose.

"That feels nice," she says, barely above a whisper.

I reach the lacy panties stretched over her feverish pussy and press one finger into her cleft, the one I licked into oblivion just days ago. I haven't stopped thinking about how she was so damn responsive when I ate her pussy, and those sounds she made… goddamn.

I want some of that for myself.

She twists in the passenger seat to face me, which positions her legs further open. Her juices are soaking through her panties, dammit, and I'm not waiting any longer and neither is she. We move toward each other so fast and hard we nearly smash noses. The result is a mind-blowing kiss that, instead of letting off some of the pressure and need of the evening, only adds to it.

I've kissed her before, I know, but this time it's different and it might as well be the first time, it's so hot. I guess the difference is that I *know* her now. I *like* her now.

I don't care what other guys say, it *is* different when you're into a woman.

Fuck that sensitive guy shit I always get.

She melts into me, at least as much as a person can in the front seat of a borrowed Chevy Cavalier, and rakes her fingers through my hair. I freeze because this woman has just discovered my kryptonite, and now I am well and truly screwed.

"Shit, Livvy, you don't know what that does to me," I moan.

Get it together, asshole. She's going to think you're a freak. Which is just as well. She's going or find out sooner or later, anyway.

36

ENZO

"C'MON," I say, pulling Livvy's dress back down and twisting the key from the ignition. "Let's get inside."

I start to open my door, but she places a hand on my arm. "I thought you had to get up early tomorrow," she teases.

Yeah. Funny girl.

"Well. I get up early every day, but I used that as an excuse tonight to get you away from my family before someone ate you alive."

She drops her head back, laughing, and grabs for the door handle. When I reach the sidewalk, I take her hand and we run up the front steps to her townhouse and reach the door just in time for one of her neighbors to hold it for us as he's coming out.

"Hey, Arthur," Livvy says breathlessly.

The neighbor starts to say something but we run past him and into the building so fast we don't hear him. When I look back over my shoulder, he's standing on the front stoop, his mouth hanging open.

Before Livvy can even open her apartment door, I back her up against it, my hands gripping her hair while we kiss. I press my aching hard-on into her tummy, and her quickened breath intensifies my need that much more.

I've never wanted anyone or anything as much as I do right now. If I weren't ready to fucking cream my jeans, I might actually be frightened.

In spite of ourselves, we finally spill into her apartment which, to be honest, I don't even take a look at. I can't take my eyes off the pretty girl before me, and how nice her dress is going to look when it comes off her.

But she's fast and makes quick work of pulling my polo over my head. When she does, she takes a small step back and gasps, laying her hands on my tattoos, something that clearly surprises her.

Then, she goes in for the kill, fumbling with my belt buckle and fly. As thrilling as it is, I can't say I'm surprised. The woman runs a freaking business, after all. She's no damn shrinking violet. She's tough. She cleans dog assholes or something like that, clearly not for the faint of heart.

My cock bounces out of my boxers and I don't even

care anymore about my own clothes. I just want Livvy's off. I grab the hem of her dress and pull it up, over her head. It falls to the floor somewhere while I catch my breath, admiring the beauty before me. There she stands, in her little booties, pink lace panties, and a light blue bra.

Why do I love so much that she doesn't bother to match her underwear?

I kick off my shoes and with my pants still hanging around my hips, brush my lips down her neck and along her shoulder until I can't stand it anymore. I take a bite.

"Ouch," she chirps, more out of surprise than pain.

"Get on the sofa," I tell her while giving my cock a couple strokes. "Kneel on it. Facing away."

She does as she's told, lowering her head and raising her ass in the air without my even having to ask.

Jesus, I'm in trouble. Her ass is *primo primo*, as the guys in my neighborhood used to say, soft and smooth and flawless. Yeah, I saw it the other night, but it's mine tonight, and is, accordingly, that much more beautiful.

I reach to pull her bra below her breasts, taking my time kneading and pinching her nipples. Then, I pull her panties down her thighs, and there's my beauty, her most private parts displayed for my eyes only.

Her pussy lips protrude from between her thighs, that's how tight together her legs are, but she's arched, giving me a perfect view of everything, from her asshole down to her little clit. I drop to my knees and dive in, licking her from one end to the other.

I pull back for a moment to open her pussy, now fully drenched in her excitement. "So pretty."

I reach for her tits again with one hand and drive two fingers inside her with my other. "Yeah," I murmur, "so nice and tight."

Her head starts to buck and she pushes back as best she can, restrained by my grip. I lean close to her ear. "You like it, Livvy? You like my fingers banging your pussy?"

She grunts. "I do, Enzo. I do," she rasps.

She's so warm, actually hot, like she's encased in fever, and I'm holding her so she can scarcely move, only resist the force of my body around hers, and then she screams, her pussy tightening around my fingers, pulsing, and I realize I need to get my cock in there.

She's still moaning when I check in with her. "You good, baby?" I ask.

Her head bobs, and she sputters some version of the word *yes*.

"That's my good girl."

I position myself behind her, her legs still pressed tightly closed, and rub my cock through her moisture. "You ready?"

"Yes, Enzo, yes."

"And what are you ready for, Livvy?"

"I... I'm ready for your cock."

Goddamn.

"How do you want it, baby?"

"Soft, no, I mean hard. I don't know. Just fuck me!"

I drive inside her, all the way, without a moment of hesitation, vaguely hoping she's really up for a hard fucking. From the sounds she's making, looks like we're on the same page.

"God, Enzo," she moans, "yes. Just like that."

She bucks back against me, so hard she's almost breaking my dick, and from the side, I can see her pretty tits bouncing. I hold still for a moment to let her do the driving and when her pace increases, there's a roar in my balls that surges to my dick.

"Oh fuck, I'm gonna come. God, baby, this is perfect. You're perfect."

With one last pump, I explode inside her, coming so hard I can't see and need to hold onto her hips to remain upright.

Her pussy tightens around me one more time and I pulse inside her, still hard, until she comes again.

I'm not sure how we make it off the sofa, or clean up, or end up in the bedroom. I only know when it's morning because the alarm on my Apple watch goes off and I know I'll be wearing a smile all day.

37

LIVVY

Damn. What did Enzo do to me last night?

I wake up to the sun broiling my bedroom, a problem I usually avoid thanks to my Ikea black-out curtains. I always, always close them before I turn in for the night because they block out not only unwanted light but also a lot of street noise.

Well, I close them except for the nights I get ravaged by a hot chef.

Like last night.

Now I'm lying in a puddle of sweat, my mouth dry and eyes scratchy, and when I reach for my phone to check the time, my back screams, probably from arching with my ass in the air for so long. The pillow next to mine smells of Enzo, slightly spicy, maybe from his deodorant or something, and the simple smell of basic soap.

What the hell. It was totally worth it, back pain, blinding light, and all.

Enzo is nowhere to be seen, probably either gone to work or maybe just done with me now that we played hide the sausage.

I try a couple stretches I learned in yoga to loosen my lower back, checking my phone at the same time because I'm efficient that way, and find no fewer than a dozen text messages from Arthur.

Cripes, did someone die?

As I scroll through them, another one comes in.

> Dammit girl, fucking wake up and call me!

Each text is a variation on the same. I don't have to be a brain surgeon to know he's dying for some scoop on last night.

> Just woke up. Can't talk.

> No way, bitch. I want the dirt NOW.

> Later

> Fine. You're selfish. I'm at work. Call me here.

There's nothing else of interest on my phone, including no declaration of love from Enzo, nor a friendly little text saying good morning, so I crawl out of bed, suck down a couple Aleve pills, and get in a very hot shower.

Holy shit. I fucked Enzo.

And Arthur knows I did, which means everyone else in the world will know by the end of the day.

I could ask him to keep his mouth shut but that would be as useless as a one-legged man in an ass-kicking contest. The only thing left to do at this point is damage control. Which I actually have no idea how to do.

So I do nothing.

Oh, I'm such an idiot.

I mean, sure, it was great to get some nook-nook, and doing it with a hunk like Enzo made it about a thousand times hotter.

But really, Livvy?

What am I doing messing around with guys from the business next door? When things go south—and they will—I'll have to see them on the regular.

Well, assuming I still have a business next door to them.

Why couldn't I just hook up with some guy from the West Side, whose path I would never cross again? There's something like one-and-a-half million people in Manhattan. Divided in half, that gives me over seven hundred thousand men to choose from.

And I end up with the guys from next door. Maybe I should just stick with the creeps my sister introduces me to. That way, if I fuck them, I can pretty easily avoid them afterward, should I need to.

I arrive at the shop, where it's reeking of weed, and I am so not in the mood.

I plop my stuff on the counter and put my hands on my hips. "Jewel, did you get high inside the store again? Dammit, I thought you were going to stick with the edibles."

She waves away my concerns, which of course only pisses me off more.

"First of all, you know cannabis is for my anxiety, and it's legal here now, so you can't deny me."

I squeeze my eyes tight. "I'm not denying you anything, Jewel—"

"But listen, Livvy, Mrs. Johnson came in to shop and her chubby dog took a dump. The pot smell covers it up beautifully." She beams, waiting for me to praise her for her brilliant thinking.

I sigh. It's pointless. "Did you clean it up, Jewel?"

Yes, I actually need to ask her this, because on more than one occasion she's left a pile of dog crap for me to clean, claiming the task is not in her job description.

We don't have job descriptions.

"Yes. I did," she sniffs. "You know it's a violation of health code not to."

Wow. She's finally listening to me.

"Thank you," I say, chafing that I have to thank her at all. "You stay up here for awhile, okay?"

I head to the back of the shop, forced to navigate a

gauntlet of empty cardboard boxes, the removal of which Jewel also must believe is not in her job description. I drop my things right there and noisily break them all down because I'm in a shitty passive-aggressive mood, and stagger out the back door to drop them in the recycling bin in the alley.

And who do I run into there, but Enzo, breaking down boxes himself.

"Oh. Hi." I say.

Dammit. I so did not want to see him.

Despite my grouchiness, his face lights up. Yeah, I guess you do that for a girl who lets you do her doggy-style.

He looks around to make sure we're alone. "Good morning. I hope I didn't wake you when I left."

"Nope. Not at all."

You also didn't wake me with a good morning text asking me how I am, nor thanking me for leaving the city last night for dinner with your family.

I turn to head back into Pawsh Pets.

"Hey, where're you running off to?" he asks, still smiling.

Damn him. One thick, black curl hangs down his forehead, and his deep-set green eyes sparkle in the day's sunshine.

I throw him a glance over my shoulder. "Got a lot to do," I mumble.

I pull the door closed behind me but not before I see him still standing there, confusion splashed across his face, frozen in place like he doesn't know what to do.

I don't know what to do either, but I'm not doing my thinking in a stinky alley next to the cardboard recycling.

38

LIVVY

I SETTLE into my mess of an office and lean back in my chair. I just want a moment to catch my breath and convince myself I'm not the biggest bitch on earth because I just blew off Enzo.

But Jewel pops her head in. "Livvy? Are you busy?"

I want to scream that I'm always busy and doesn't she fucking see that? But hey, I'm not *that* big of a bitch.

"I forgot to tell you something." She cautiously approaches my desk, finally having picked up on my shit mood, and tosses a piece of paper in front of me. She turns and runs out.

I pull the wrinkled, dirty page in front of me. It's a plain white piece of printer paper that someone thoughtfully sent me a message on.

> *Your fight is futile.*
> *Cooperate before you are forced to.*

What? Is this some sort of fucking joke?

If my looming bankruptcy—let's face it, that's about what it's come down to— wasn't a bad enough nightmare, then this is the haunting that's sure to drive me over the edge.

Am I just trying to keep my business alive? Or do I need to add myself to the list?

I run to the front of the store. "Where did you find this? Where did it come from?"

Jewel shrinks down in her chair. "Um, well, it was taped to the door. I'm sorry I didn't give it to you when you first came in."

"Fuckers..." I mumble, while chills rush over my skin.

"Who... who's it from, Livvy?"

"Good question. I want to know who it's from too. So I can kick the living shit out of their asses."

Something inside me detonates and I blast out the front door, marching right over to EastSide.

I walk right up to the first guy I see, Owen, who's talking to some diners.

"Did you see this?" I demand, holding it up in his face.

He smiles, gently pushing my hand down, and excuses himself from his guests. "If it's what I think it is, then yes," he says, continuing to smile. "Weston's up in the office if you want to go talk to him. I can't do this right now."

He walks toward some other diners who've just arrived, shaking their hands and patting them on the back.

Fine. I get it. The man's busy with lunch rush. So I storm through the restaurant and up the back stairs to Weston's office.

I knock on the door. "Weston? You in there? It's me, Livvy."

"Hey, come in," he calls.

I fling the door open and his eyebrows rise as he picks up on my sense of panic. And anger. And all that shit.

I thrust the warning in his face. With a glance at it, he nods, and picks his own up off his desk. The guys got the same exact warning on the same exact kind of paper.

I'm not sure whether I'm relieved to see I'm not alone, or sorry these guys are having to confront the same. I'm so bunged up now with overwhelm, I wouldn't know logic if it hit me in the face.

"Have a seat, Livvy."

I do as he says, because I don't know what else to do.

He taps an expensive-looking pen on the desk in front of him. "Guess they don't like how we're fighting back, huh?" he says with a chuckle.

"Glad you think it's funny," I snap. "Nobody knows

what it's like to see something you've bled for teeter on its edge."

Weston's head snaps back on his neck. "Livvy, what do you think the restaurant is?" he asks indignantly.

"Oh. Well, you guys have each other. You have investors. You're not as vulnerable as I am."

He tilts his head. "I see. Well, first of all, I don't think we need to have a contest over who has it the hardest here. What we need to do is stick together."

Ha. That's *all I have to do*? Dude has no idea that each bill that comes into Pawsh Pets is another implication that I have no right to be running a business. As of this morning, I've missed a payment to a key supplier and my landlord's 'friendly reminders' of my overdue rent are becoming less friendly.

The door blows open and Owen and Enzo join us. Enzo looks at me with those same eyes he did in the alley, and I look away before I blush.

Oh, what the hell. The other guys probably know what we did anyway. They probably go over their conquests in their morning meetings.

I can see it now…

"Guys, I fucked Livvy last night."

High-fives all around.

"Dude, way to go. You gonna see her again?"

"Hell no. You know there are over seven hundred thousand women just on the little island of Manhattan…"

"Livvy. Earth to Livvy." Owen snaps his fingers in my face.

"Oh. Yeah. Sorry," I mumble.

Weston lays his pen down, thank God, because the tapping was driving me crazy. "I was just telling Livvy we received the same note she did and she feels her challenges are paramount to ours."

Wow. So he wants to play that way?

Owen jumps in. "Livvy, we're trying to be your lifebuoy with our support and friendship."

For a second I feel like a shit. But only for a second. I'm too pissed and too busy feeling sorry for myself to be gracious. Or human. Or civil.

I jump to my feet. "I have to get back."

I squeeze past Enzo and Owen, who reaches for my arm. I wriggle away from him and burst out the door, running all the way back to Pawsh Pets, once my oasis, my nirvana, and now my prison.

39

LIVVY

I GET BACK JUST in time to find Jewel packing her stuff and throwing her bag over her shoulder.

I take a deep breath. I've been enough of a bitch for the day. "Heading out?" I ask, trying to sound all cool and casual, but instead, squeaking like I'm trying too hard.

"Um, yeah," Jewel says, giving me wide berth.

Fuck, does she think I'm going to hit her or something?

"See you tomorrow?" I throw out as a peace offering.

She nods vigorously. "Yes. Yes of course. I just thought I'd tell you me and my boyfriend got back together. I'm going over his place to celebrate." She gives me the kind of smile that someone who thinks maybe they shouldn't be smiling gives.

"Ok, that's awesome. Have fun, Jewel. See you tomorrow."

She grimaces at me and is gone.

I put my hands on my hips and look around Pawsh, at the light colors, flattering light, and displays that look like something out of an expensive department store. I so carefully curated everything here, and am happy to have some time to myself with my baby, which I've so lovingly cared for since her inception.

Goddammit, I want to rage. I want to rage that this is a fucking awesome little boutique that I put my blood, sweat, and tears into and that everyone should love it the way I do.

Instead, I'm afloat in a sinking ship and I realize I'd better take a good hard look at whatever the developer is offering, with or without the cooperation of the guys next door.

Regret churns in my stomach for being so rude to them, but the truth is, it's better to cut off contact now rather than later. Sure, I've messed around with them from one degree to another, but that will just have to be my one 'wild girl' story, something Arthur tells me everyone needs at least one of.

Besides, when the guys find out what a sinking ship Pawsh is, will they really be willing to tether themselves to it? To me?

'Course not. They'll be out of here like their asses are on fire.

I suppose working with the developer rather than against him is a coward's escape. But it's an escape nonetheless, and sometimes that's what a girl needs. And yet, acceptance of their help, or should I say interference, would be the nail in the coffin of the person I believed myself to be.

I slump into the stool behind the cash wrap counter where Jewel usually sits, and feel myself breaking down into a pile of elements, rather than being a whole, healthy person. Every conflict, internal and external, is pulling me to pieces, leaving me not only at war with myself but also the whole fucking world.

I'm realizing saving Pawsh, or letting it go, is not just about my small business. I'm now facing holding together the pieces of my crumbling life.

40

OWEN

THE DAY after Livvy stormed the restaurant, we guys regroup and talk about next steps.

Would the warning she received, the one we got as well, be enough to scare her off? Is she getting closer to throwing in the towel?

And what about us? What the fuck are we supposed to do?

I look around EastSide as people start arriving for lunch service. Our bookings are down today, strange for a Thursday, but hell, every business has its ebbs and flows. I greet our usual customers, providing the extra welcome that keeps them coming back. Everything else is perking along beautifully, like the well-oiled machine that we are.

The kitchen is humming, the hosts are seating guests, the food is perfect, and the soft sound of people talking and laughing, combined with the clatter of dishes and silverware, are music to my ears.

Another perfect day in EastSide-land, what every restauranteur dreams of. I'm not even annoyed when I have to run out and get a new batch of menus printed for the dinner service because we were missing some obscure ingredient.

On my way out, I spot Livvy behind the counter at Pawsh. I catch her eye and she brightens, but only for a moment.

What's that all about?

I poke my head in anyway. "Yo, Liv. How's it hanging?"

I look around. The place is deathly quiet. It's a shame, because it's a beautiful little boutique. When I have more time, I'll have to pick some new things out for Cheddar.

The cat that isn't mine.

"Hey, Owe," she says in a flat voice. Damn if she doesn't look like she has the weight of the world on her shoulders.

Well, shit. If she's this down in the dumps, I can't just walk by like a giant douche.

The orange shop cat looks up from his nap, hisses, and jumps to the floor to run to the back of the shop.

"It's okay, Harry," Livvy says, calling after him. "Owen's okay."

I'm *okay*? Just *okay*?

Not easily defeated, I forge on. "Livvy, why don't you stop by later, after you close? At least for a drink or something. The bartender's come up with a new cocktail made of hemp-infused vodka, organic pressed green juice, and an edible flower garnish. Or something like that. He's all excited about it. Sounds right up your alley."

She gives me a half-hearted smile. "Oh, I don't know. I'm kind of tired, what with everything that's going on. And that Bartlett Murray stopped by earlier, nosing around."

Oh. Shit. "Did you let on our suspicions?"

"I wanted to. Actually, I wanted to pour my dirty dog-washing water over his head. But I didn't do that, either."

There's something awkward between us, but I don't know what it is.

"What did he want?"

"You know how he is. Just 'wanted to see how things were going,' like he always does. I just smiled and stayed polite."

Fuck me if this woman isn't in a bad way. I walk around the counter to hug her, if she'll let me. When I do, she quickly shuffles a bunch of papers around, but not before I get a glimpse of them.

Funny thing is, had she not touched them, my eye never would have been drawn toward them.

She'd made a handwritten list called 'debts,' and at the bottom of the disturbingly long list is a total.

Twenty-five thousand dollars.

Whoa.

Now, twenty-five thousand dollars of debt is not that much for a lot of businesses. EastSide carries more than that. But we have backers and steady income.

From the looks of Pawsh Pets, that's not so much the case.

Holy crap. She's dealing with this, on top of threats from the developer. I don't blame her for being down in the dumps. Hell, I would be too.

I want to help. I'm not sure how I can, but I know I have to proceed carefully. Livvy is proud, and I know what that's like. I've been down on my luck before, myself, and the last thing I wanted when I was there was any pity.

When I was a kid and word got out my dad had split and that my mom and I were just squeaking by, I swear that every look I got, from my friends' parents to the teachers at school, was the same every time they saw me.

Poor Owen, it screamed from a mile away.

I can't do the same to Livvy.

I playfully nudge her. "C'mon. Say you'll come by. Someone's got to tell us how that new cocktail is, because I sure as hell am not gonna try it."

She laugh-snorts, which I count as a major victory. "Yeah. Okay. But only for one drink."

I kiss her temple just because I feel like it, and head for the door.

Enzo told us what happened between him and Livvy. I can't say I'm not jealous. And that's not only because he got to ravish her, it's also because he just got to spend a shitload of time with her, one-on-one.

But hey, if it's meant to be, I'll have my chance too. And if she's not down with it, I'm okay with that.

"Owen, before you go, there's one thing I've been meaning to bring up."

Her tone perks up a bit. Is the old Livvy back?

"Yeah? What's up, beautiful?"

She looks down at her hands for a moment, then raises her gaze. "When Bartlett was here, he said something that confused me."

I walk back up to the counter. "What's that?"

Her eyebrows draw together, creating the cutest wrinkles on her forehead. "He said something about being aware of the developer's plans long before he let me know. He said you were aware of them too."

Oh. That.

I shuffle my feet and my mouth gets dry.

I've wondered if this was going to come out.

And when.

"I… I did know something early on. I didn't know much, though."

Fuck, that sounds lame.

She half-laughs. "Um, well, there isn't much to know. I mean, either the developer wants to take over or doesn't. But you kept that to yourself. Didn't share it with me. I had to come to you guys."

"Listen, Livvy, I wanted to tell you, but we were all just getting to know you and things kind of took on a life of their own."

She crosses her arms and, if looks could kill, I'd be six feet under.

Can't say I blame her.

And now I'm the biggest dick in the world.

"Look, I heard what sounded like a rumor. I didn't think it was true until you confirmed it. I felt like an idiot for not taking it more seriously, and I didn't speak up. I wasn't trying to pull anything over on you. Really."

She sighs and stacks the papers on the counter into a neat pile, fastening them with a paperclip. Then she moves over to the wall where cat food is displayed and begins straightening the cans.

I take that as my cue to leave. "I hope you'll stop by tonight, Livvy. We'd really like to see you."

She doesn't say a word, just waves over her shoulder. I really want to stick around and continue to my attempt to smooth things out, but I've got to get the damn menus and get back to the restaurant.

Maybe she just needs some time.

I leave, the bells on the door screeching into the silence.

I hustle down to the printer and drop a bag of charcoal matcha macarons on the counter in front of my contact there. She's wearing her badge today, for a change.

"Ellen! How's it going?" I ask, taking the menus from her.

She looks from side to side, leaning over the counter toward me. "Owen, I have to tell you something," she says in a low voice.

Holy shit. What could be so serious? She's on a diet and doesn't want my treats anymore?

"What's up?"

She looks around again, apparently about to tell me something she shouldn't. "When you get out of the store, look at the document on top of the menus. I can't say any more."

With that, she grabs her macarons, stuffs them in her apron pocket, and gets back to work.

Jesus. What's all the drama about? She used the wrong paper for the menus?

I get outside the printshop and walk a couple store fronts down the street. If what she's telling me is so top-secret, I guess I'd better be discreet until I know what the hell is going on.

I reach into the large envelope holding the night's dinner menus and see the top page is indeed different from the menus, in both color and size. I slide it out and turn it around to find a photocopy of a restaurant review from today's paper.

A review of EastSide.

41

OWEN

AT THE START of its meteoric ascent to the top of hip, new dining establishments in the City, EastSide didn't just push culinary boundaries, it catapulted them to previously unexplored dimensions, earning them the prime spot as poster child of avant-garde cuisine.

But time marches on and just as we age, so do restaurants. What was once an electrifying dining experience at EastSide has now become, at best, a low hum.

Today, their dishes seem reminiscent of their glorious past, but are now lacking a certain spark. The intricate dance of flavors is still there, but feels rehearsed, no longer spontaneous, surprising, or delighting, which once made EastSide so unique. While a few stalwarts are still reminders of the restaurant's zenith, they are now just islands amidst mediocrity.

And it's not just the food. The service, once a seamless dance of precision, is now disjointed. The wait between courses can be lengthy, and the servers look flustered.

I'm happy to say all is not lost. The wine list, curated with a creative and discerning eye, still offers a robust, eclectic, if not expensive selection.

As I'm sure we all do, I remain hopeful that EastSide, with some serious reflection and rejuvenation, may be able to reignite its former flame. To do this, it would do well to study other failed culinary darlings of the City, dissecting their downfall, while forging ahead with the renewed, daring spirit that once set it apart. The three young men running East-Side, all very nice guys, have many years in the restaurant business ahead of them. Let's hope it doesn't all end here.

But as we know, I've been reviewing eating establishments in the City for a long time. Can restaurants recover from a fall into tedium? I can safely say rarely, if ever.

Time will tell if EastSide can fight its way back to the spotlight that made it an instant success. For now, we remember and hope.

As soon as I'm back in the restaurant, I find Weston in the kitchen and thrust the review in his face. "What's this?" he asks, turning the page upright. "Oh, I haven't seen the paper yet today."

But as he skims the article and realizes what it is,

his eyes get dark. Before he's even done reading, he looks like he's ready to punch someone or something.

"What the fucking fuck?" he roars.

Every head in the kitchen turns our way, and I'm relieved we're not having this conversation out in the dining room in front of customers.

Enzo joins us and reads the review. When he finishes, he explodes with a litany of swear words.

He's crushed. Just absolutely crushed. While we all run the restaurant with equal weight on our shoulders, this is no doubt the biggest blow to Enzo, whose menu designs are his pride and joy.

If I could have handled this without involving him, I would have. Mister-wears-his-emotions-on-his-sleeve takes stuff like this hard.

"What the fuck, Owe? Where'd you get this? Why is it a photocopy?" he asks.

"When I went to pick up tonight's menus, the girl at the printer shop told me she'd slipped something into the package. She was cagey, like she'd get in trouble or something for doing it. When I got outside, I found this article with a note she'd attached that someone had come in and had one thousand copies printed off."

Enzo looks like he's going to get sick. He grabs a chair and drops his head into his hands. I put a hand on his shoulder, like that's going to help.

Now, not only is everyone in the kitchen trying to eavesdrop, they are also inching closer, hoping to find out what the drama is all about. I don't blame them.

"Guys, get back to work," Enzo hollers, like he has eyes in the back of his head.

Weston groans, rubbing his temples. "What's the fucking deal here? Why the shit review and why would anyone make a thousand copies of it?"

I say what we all already know. "If you make a thousand copies of something, that means you are going to distribute it. It's that simple."

But distribute to whom? And why?

Enzo pounds his fist on the stainless-steel prep table. "How in the fuck did this happen? The critics love us. At least, they used to."

It's true. We've gotten nothing but the highest praise since the day we opened. What changed? Not to say we've ever rested on our laurels—that's not how we roll—but did we take something for granted? Have we slipped?

Is this the reason our bookings are down today? And for the rest of the week?

Something flip-flops in my stomach and I, too, pull up a chair next to Enzo.

Weston paces. "Guys, something about this doesn't smell right. You don't go from being at the top of the heap one day to the bottom the next. This is suspicious."

"Do you... do you think someone 'encouraged' the restaurant critic to write this?" I ask quietly, with air quotes around 'encouraged.'

I almost don't say it out loud because I don't want

to believe it's possible. Aren't journalists supposed to be objective? Above influence?

Or I am a fucking naïve idiot? The only one who doesn't know how the game is played.

I look to Weston. Enzo and I both do. He's been immersed in the business world since before he could walk, and we often turn to him with our questions.

He nods slowly. "I wouldn't be surprised. Someone wants this city block badly. Badly enough that they are willing to pay off people, like the slimeball who wrote this. It's just too much of a coincidence."

"I... I didn't think much of it, and didn't think to mention it, guys, but our bookings today are down. And they are for the rest of the week."

"Why didn't you say anything?" Enzo asks.

I shrug. "I thought it was, you know, just one of the ups and downs any restaurant sees. But... maybe not."

Fury crosses Weston's face. "Fucking dirtbags. The sooner they damage our business, the sooner we'll hit the road."

I consider sharing my exchange with Livvy and decide I've delivered enough bad news of the day. But my concerns about her are weighing on me. "By the way, I poked my head into Pawsh Pets on the way to the printer. Livvy had some papers she didn't want me to see, but I did anyway. She's in debt. A lot of debt, at least for her."

"Maybe they're fucking with her business too," Enzo says.

Weston shakes his head "It's not a maybe. It's a definite."

I glance at my watch. "Hey, it's time for the dinner service. We gotta hold it together. Freak out later."

Enzo looks around the kitchen and claps his hands loudly. "All right, everybody. Back to work."

42

OWEN

I CAN'T SAY it was easy to dive into dinner service with a smile on my face after reading that shitty review, and even worse, realizing it was dishonestly written.

Nothing prepared me for this. Nor the guys. Weston, who has more of a business background than any of us, says shit like this goes down all the time in the business world. He just didn't see it coming our way.

I mean, who would?

I half-heartedly greet some neighborhood regulars who pat my arm with a kind 'everything will be okay.' So, the word is out. People have read about us and are now talking about us.

There's so fucking much at stake. Not just the business, but the friendship among us guys, our commitment to our investors, and the neighborhood.

Our budding relationship with Livvy. Although she has her own shit sandwich she's dealing with.

Things could either bloom, and we come out on top smelling like fucking roses, or crash and burn, leaving everything, including our reputations, in tatters. We guys haven't had the chance to discuss approaches to this latest development, but I'd bet a month's salary we'll each have different ideas on what our next move should be.

That'll be fun.

The worst of it is that a bad restaurant review is like a death spiral. Diners stay away because they want to believe they are as discerning as the famous critic whose word is gospel. Suppliers get nervous they won't get paid and tighten up credit. Staff start looking for new jobs, anticipating layoffs. And shit keeps falling apart piece by piece until there's a critical mass of destruction like in a Jenga game.

I'm fighting my pessimistic nature, but it's not doing any good. In my experience, when the future is looking shitty, there's a reason for it. No amount of 'hoping' or 'sending good vibes' makes damn bit of difference.

There is one thing that will brighten my mood, although that's as uncertain as everything else in my life right now. But I can't help it. Everybody needs something to brighten their day. I look at my watch.

Livvy should be walking through the door any minute.

I have the bartender save her a seat at the bar and have one of the kitchen staff whip up a little egg and artichoke frittata. I figure the longer I can ply her with food and drink, the longer she'll stick around. She's got to know I wasn't purposely keeping information from her. She knows I wouldn't do that.

Right?

I'm craning my neck to see out the door from my vantage point at the back of the dining room. When it flies open, I look for my lovely guest. Instead, three dressed-to-kill women saunter in like they own the place, sashaying across the room, right up to me.

"Hello, handsome," one says.

The one named Kristyll—that's how she spells it— throws an overly-perfumed arm around my neck and kisses my cheek before I can duck out of the way, no doubt leaving a huge smear of red lipstick behind. Before she releases me, she presses her fake tits into my arm to make sure I didn't miss the cleavage revealed by her low-cut blouse.

The other two, Adrena and Shay, do the same, each one getting a bit more familiar than the one before. Normally, I'm okay with flirts like this, but today, not so much. I've got too much on my mind to flatter these women the way they expect.

Park of their march through the restaurant and overly friendly display of affection is for attention gathering, and it's worked beautifully. Everyone, while too polite to stare, has noticed them, and the ladies are reveling in the attention.

Problem is, some people notice them who I wish hadn't.

Like Livvy.

She stands at the front door, frozen in place, watching the women fawn over me.

She'll know it's just normal friendliness, right?

Wrong.

She frowns. Maybe she's confused. At the same time, one of the women hooks her arm through mine, laughing and talking while I walk them to their table. Before they sit, one of them goes as far as running a finger down my chest, purring about something stupid.

When I finally break away, Livvy's backing toward the door. I wave, gesturing her to come in, but her face transforms from confused to hurt. And just like that, she's out the door and gone.

Goddammit.

I start to run after her but one of the diners catches my arm to ask for more water. Annoyed, I look around for the bussing staff and see no one in sight. I refill all the water glasses that I can see needing it, wondering if the restaurant critic was on to something.

Has our service slipped? How were these diners left without a drop of water for the majority of their meal?

I finish, but by the time I manage to go after Livvy,

she's long gone. Pawsh is lights out and locked up. I don't even see her walking down the street.

How'd she disappear so fast?

Fuck, fuck, fuck.

With a pit in my stomach the size of the Grand Canyon, I force a fake-ass smile and get back inside EastSide like a good showman whose business is on the line and who will do anything to save it.

43

LIVVY

I SLURPED my last ramen noodle, the broth dribbling down my white blouse.

And I don't even care.

On the way home from work I got takeout from the place around the corner. I'd planned on having a nice dinner and fancy cocktail at EastSide, having been convinced to stop in by Owen, but when I saw some of his customers looking *very* friendly with him, I lost my appetite.

Fuck those people. All of them. Fuck the bistro boys, with their weird-ass food and organic everything, and fuck their beautiful patrons with their Botoxed faces, wearing the latest fashions from Barney's.

Wait, Barney's went out of business. At least I think

it did. Truth is, I don't even know where those New York glamazons get their high-fashion clothes. Whatever. Let them waste their time and money competing with each other and for the likes of men like Owen, Weston, and Enzo. They can have them, all of them.

Talk about adding insult to injury.

I know I'm not like other women in New York. I'm not hip, cute, or popular. Never have been, never will be. But I love it here, starting with my tiny apartment within walking distance of everything. And my boutique providing cool stuff to dedicated pet owners. Even my crazy employee, Jewel, and my buddy, Arthur. I enjoy Mrs. Perkins too, whose dog is still not properly potty trained even though he's four years old.

I love every minute of the life I've created for myself. I'm not like my sister, who picks her friends based on what they can do for her and her husband. I don't fit in with the guys they try to introduce me to, all carbon copies of each other, the only difference among them their names and their hairlines.

Those women cozying up to Owen—I know their type. They're the mean girls. They hate everyone who's not them. Hell, they probably even hate each other. To them, the world is a zero-sum game, and anyone— including their closest friends—who gets something they don't, is taking away what they feel they deserve. One of their best friends starts dating a nice guy? She's mad he didn't pick *her* instead.

I may never have been part of that crowd, but I've

been an observer of it. I know how they operate. They're not nice. And I want no part of them.

Including the type of men they pursue. They're all the same, those people

I never should have gotten involved with any of the guys from EastSide. I don't care that Enzo looks after his nonna, Owen practically had to raise himself, and Weston's on the outs with his rich family.

They can suck it.

Everything was good for a while. And now I'm plummeting over the cliff of life, with down the only way to go. Soon, I'll crash land at the bottom of the canyon, breaking into a million pieces with all the other losers who never got their shit together.

Next morning, I wake up late and drag my ass to the shop because what would be the point of rushing? It's not going to change anything.

"Hey, Livvy!" Jewel chirps, opening a new shipment of Cucci dog and cat clothes.

According to the nasty letter they sent me earlier this week, this will be my last shipment from these folks until I start paying down my overdue invoices. I don't blame them, not one bit. I'd do the same.

Who wants to do business with a deadbeat who can't pay their damn bills?

"Hi Jewel. Thanks for covering for me this morning. I've been having a hard time getting motivated," I say.

I don't usually pour my heart out to Jewel, but I don't have much left to lose.

"No worries," she says, rocking in place like she hears music.

I wouldn't doubt it.

"Hey, I'm wondering if I can take off a bit early today. My mom's coming to take me to dinner," she says. "I haven't seen her in ages."

Glad somebody has something to look forward to.

"Sure. Where're you going?"

She claps her hands together, bouncing up and down in her Converse Chucks. "EastSide!"

What? Did she just say EastSide? The business next door that's become the bane of my existence?

She mistakes the surprise on my face for excitement.

"I know, right? Their prix-fixe dinner is five hundred dollars a head. I'd never go there if not for my mom." Her gaze snaps my way as she corrects herself. "Or an event we're invited to. Ya know?"

Yeah. I know. I can't afford to fucking eat there either, having enjoyed the place only when the guys took pity on me and plied me with free stuff, probably leftovers, or food that was expired.

Yuck.

You can't trust anyone who's not a vegetarian.

44

LIVVY

THE FRONT DOORBELL jingles and for the first time ever, I suppress a groan. I am not in the mood to deal with the public, even if they're spending money that is vital to my survival. I just want to go back home and crawl under the covers. Maybe eat those stale saltines in the back of my kitchen cupboard. Pretty soon, that's all I'll be able to afford.

I look up to see Tim the parrot guy walk in with his dirty-mouthed bird on his shoulder. I brace myself for it to say something about my tits, but it's much more interested in Harry the cat, who's sizing him up.

"Hello, Lovely Livvy," Tim booms.

Cripes, he's always so happy.

He puts on a fake-stern face. "I didn't see you at my

comedy show, Livvy. You should have been there, what with the coupon I got for ya. I killed it up there onstage, Livvy, I really did. You should have heard the laughter. The applause."

Behind him, Jewel is rolling her eyes so hard I don't know how they stay in her head. But truth be told, his joy is so authentic I'm happy for him. I really am. It's nice to see good things happened in the world, even if they're not for me.

I'm not so bitter I can't be happy for another person.

"Oh, Tim, that's so awesome, I'm glad it went well. And I'm sorry I missed it," I say, trying to shake off the heavy feeling weighing me down.

He cocks his head. "Say, are you okay? Coming down with something?"

Now I feel like a jerk. The guy might be a huge dork, but he's never been anything but nice to me, unlike the creeps next door. And his concern now is just so… kind, when I've written him off time and again. Even if his bird does talk about my tits.

"I… I have a lot on my mind, Tim. There's so much going on," I say in a tired voice.

I need to perk it up. I mean, he's a freaking customer. He doesn't need to see me losing my shit.

"Oh. Of course. Like that developer nonsense? Yeah, that really sucks. But isn't all the support you pulled together at Wine & Whiskers making a difference? I thought you had the whole neighborhood on your side."

His bird craps down the back of his shirt and he doesn't notice. Jewel does though and jumps back several feet.

"Yeah, I think people are on my side, but that only goes so far. I'm still hoping for help from the city, but it seems like when a developer has deep enough pockets, they can do anything they want."

He reaches out and touches my hand, which I really appreciate. I just needed one person to be nice to me today.

"Livvy, if there's anything I can do, please let me know. I know it must be extra hard with Bartlett Murray's connection to the developer. I don't know how you will overcome that."

Wait. What? I knew Bartlett had some connection to them, but never managed to get any details.

I proceed carefully. "How is Bartlett connected with that group?" I ask casually.

He picks up his parrot treats and puts them on the counter to pay. "Oh, you know, the developer happens to be his brother-in-law. Rumor has it he's already helped them get plans approved and permits started."

No fucking way.

Tim must have seen the confusion on my face. "Oh, Livvy. Make no mistake, these people are moving fast."

"I… I…" For a moment, I can't form words. "I didn't know he was related to them… that they're family."

Tim nods vigorously. "Oh yeah. Everyone knows that. Thought you did too. But you're fighting them, right? It'd be a shame for you to leave. Same with the guys next door. So, anyway, look, I have another coupon for my next show at the comedy club. I hope you can make it this time."

He pulls out a credit card and pays for his stuff.

"I'll try, Tim. I really will. And thank you for the kind support."

A lump builds in my throat, and Jewel sees that I'm about to have a mini-breakdown. She takes me by the arm and guides me to my desk so I can emote in private. She pats me on the cheek before she leaves, which is funny because she's the employee and I'm the boss. Her kindness pushes me over the edge and a sob escapes my throat. She helps me to my chair, and quietly closes the office door on her way out.

I try to bargain with the universe. Tell it I'm not asking for much. I want just enough to keep the shop going and pay my bills. It's fine that other people have it easier than me, have more than me, it really is. I don't have big dreams. I haven't gone through life with a sense of entitlement. I've worked hard, made my own opportunities, and never taken advantage of anyone. I've kept my mouth shut and my chin up at life's little insults. The big insults too. I never bit back, and God knows I've had cause to.

In the midst of my meltdown, I see a call coming in from Owen.

Great. Just who I want reminding me of my mediocrity, and the merciful attentions he and the guys paid me when they thought there was something to be gained from it. I fell for their flattery, their good food, their handsome faces. I thought for a moment I was in the club. The club I'd never been invited to before.

Come to find out, I was given a taste, allowed in the front door, and just as I was liking it, found myself on the outside looking in. Again. Like I always am.

I can see it now, the three of them in their perfect restaurant with their perfect lives, laughing about the 'sad girl next door.' Isn't it nice of them to pay a girl like me some attention when my sort is surely starved of not only male affection, but also the sort of graces guys like that are granted on a daily basis.

I'm angry. I'll show them. I don't know how, but I'll find a way.

I could burn their place down. But that might burn mine too. And while highly illegal, that might solve some of my problems. Cash in on my insurance? Leave town?

Yeah, I'd leave town in an orange jumpsuit on my way to Riker's Island.

I could let loose a horde of rats or cockroaches that would keep their diners away.

I could spread a rumor that I'd gotten horrible food poisoning there.

Or I could just ignore them. Forever. Or for at least as long as both our businesses are here.

Yeah, that's the most likely option.

45

LIVVY

"Why aren't you returning my calls?"

"I am now. What can I do for you?" I ask in a tired voice.

I am tired. So tired. Of everything.

Owen exhales a long breath. "Livvy, I know you're not happy with me right now, but I want you to believe me when I say I wasn't trying to pull one over on you by not telling you when I first got wind of the developer plans. I honestly thought it would come to nothing. You know how people in this city like to speculate. They're always looking for an angle. An opportunity to strike it rich, usually on the back of some other poor bastard."

He finally stops talking. I think he must be out of breath.

The silence, while he waits for me to say something, is as thick as his weird celeriac sauce.

Really, did people come from all corners of the city and pay top dollar to eat some of these concoctions? Give me a vegetarian taco any day and I'm a happy girl.

Mr. Smooth continues to try to spin his way out of the doghouse. What he doesn't realize is that trust, once shattered, does not somehow just regenerate. It's crushed beyond repair, then stomped on for good measure. There's no backpedaling. He should be smart enough to realize this. He and his buddies.

"Livvy, it's true that I knew. Or rather that I'd heard. And it's true I wasn't going to tell you, way back in the beginning, anyway, before we started... getting to know you. Then, I didn't want to tell you because I didn't want you to think I was a slimy motherfucker. But we became... friends, or whatever you want to call it. I don't know what to call it, Livvy, but I'm not ready to throw it away. I hope you're not, either."

Is he serious? Does he really think he can basically just tell me to get over it and forget everything that's happened? What is it with guys like him? And Owen and Enzo? They get their way every fucking day, every fucking time they want something.

They're so used to it, they expect it. Just like Owen expects me not to throw away 'whatever it is we have.'

Which is a big fat nothing, I'll remind him.

As soon as I stop crying.

It's all such a mess. As much as I want to untangle myself from this web of deceit and half-truths, where everyone is out for themselves with no regard for me, these guys are still my best—really my *only*—chance at saving what's left of my shop.

And my life.

"I gotta go."

I end the call. I don't know what to say and I certainly don't want Owen to know how upset I am. I'm not giving him that much power over me. He already has enough.

Jewel left to meet her mother for dinner at East-Side. I try not to feel betrayed that she's supporting them because why shouldn't she? They make food that people like. She's going to have a nice dinner with her mother. Who's also paying for it.

I look out the front window of Pawsh. I'm going to miss this view, of a moderately busy Manhattan side street with a mini-mart on the corner, a dry cleaner next to it, and various other neighborhood conveniences scattered throughout. I'll even miss the abandoned shoe store directly across the street, which already has a prospective tenant, I've heard through the rumor mill.

I wander around my once-thriving boutique, now a monument to crushed dreams and broken trust. My phone buzzes—another text from Owen—but I ignore it.

I can't. I just can't.

I'm evaluating everything—not just my failed marketing strategies but also the so-called 'relationships' I fell into with the guys next door. Should I stick with the once-allies who turned out to be only marginally honest? Or pull on my big girl panties and go solo? Can I be my own David and slay the dreadful Goliath?

46

WESTON

THERE IS no kiss of death for a restaurant like a bad review, especially one from an influential critic who can sink ships with the flick of a pen. Whoever planted ours knows that well and didn't hesitate to use it against us.

Bastards.

And the fucker who wrote the piece is no better. In fact, he's worse.

We did everything right. We followed all the rules. We raised enough money. We weren't assholes to anyone as we climbed our way to success.

Yet, we were still vulnerable. How the hell does that happen?

Actually, I don't have to ask. I've seen it. Lived it.

My father's businesses were on both the receiving and delivering end of both of those all the time. If I were to ask Dad, which I would not give him the pleasure of, he'd say it's just another day at the office. That if I thought we guys here at EastSide were immune to the ugly side of commerce, I was naïve as hell and apparently never learned a thing from him.

As Dad would say, in the business world, someone is always getting fucked, and someone is always doing the fucking.

Yup, I guess I am naïve.

I have no right to be surprised the developer resorted to playing dirty. Why wouldn't he? People want what they want and will take opportunities when they see them.

I look around the restaurant, having emerged from my office, resisting the temptation to hide there and let everything implode around me. Once in the dining room, I take in the lunchtime quiet. It's not that the place is silent, far from it, but when the dining room is full and chugging ahead at full-speed, like on a normal day, the hum is unmistakable. We certainly have people eating here today, but the sound of their chatter, along with clanking plates and silverware, is not at the noise level it should be. In fact, when the bartender starts up the espresso machine, it startles the crap out of me.

Our once-vibrant atmosphere, while hardly dead, is subdued. Diners won't have noticed, of course, at least I hope they haven't, but I have and it's the kind of thing that makes me ache to the bones. I have no doubt Owen and Enzo feel the same. We'll find a way to fight back, I know we will. We just have to keep our focus. And stay angry.

But if that's all we need to do, why do I feel like the captain at the helm of a sinking ship, helplessly watching it go down?

As if this isn't bad enough, our lovely friend and neighbor won't have anything to do with us. Owen's little secret got out and he seems to think she's done with us guys, like we're vectors of a contagious disease. No more partnering as we each try to save our businesses and no more… whatever you call it. It's not like we were dating her, per se, but I know I sure as hell was enjoying getting to know her better. I never thought it would come to such an abrupt halt, almost before it even got started. As if our business alliance isn't disappointing enough, our lifeline to her is snapped, broken, and unlikely to be repaired. I've reached out to her via text a couple times and been replied to with curt answers or complete radio silence. I thought of going over there for an in-person chat, but I suspect that's the last thing she wants from me.

Ever since Owen told me about the debt she's carrying, I haven't stopped worrying. I know she's worked hard, and I know what it's like to have your dream threatened. I'd hate to see Pawsh Pets go belly up. It would be a loss for the neighborhood and devastating to her.

Devastating to me.

It's like everything around me is fraying at the edges, very close to being nothing more than a hanging thread about to be snipped. Owen's drenched in guilt, which I actually think he should be, Enzo's a ball of rage, something I've never seen. And me? I'm in crisis management mode but not managing to accomplish much at all. My bond with the guys, my North Star for years, feels like it's fallen through a black hole.

What disturbs me the most? Even more than East-Side's threatened future? Losing these guys, my closest friends. My chosen family. The trust and camaraderie that used to be our superpower is now on a wobbly foundation that may not hold.

And then there's Livvy, who's becoming a stranger before I really even got to know her. She'd become more important to me that I cared to admit, and now it's too late to tell her.

Or is it?

I make a decision. I'm going over there to talk to her. If she kicks me out, fine, but it won't be because I didn't let her know how I feel.

47

WESTON

"WELL, THIS FUCKING SUCKS," Owen groans.

"What are you doing with that Japanese beer? Run out of Bud?" Enzo asks.

Owen belches and shrugs. "Too lazy to go back and get them."

Damn. And I thought I had a bad day.

I duck behind the bar, the bartender long gone for the evening, and pour myself the same beer Owen's having. Unlike him, I actually like this stuff.

"Heard about your blow up with Livvy, dude," Enzo says.

Wow. He's usually pretty diplomatic. Guess he's reached the end of his nice-guy rope. I brace myself for what's next.

"Oh yeah. What'd you hear?"

Enzo rolls his head on his neck. "Basically, that you stuck your foot in it. Pissed her off so bad she won't talk to any of us now."

Owen frowns. "Dude, you have no idea what you're talking about, so just shut it."

We're all silent for a moment. I don't know who's more stunned about Owen's smack-down, but I can safely say it's pretty fucking surprising to all of us.

"You know, if you'd just been honest from the beginning, shared what you knew, we might not be in this mess right now," Enzo adds.

Owen slams his hand on the bar. "Right, Enzo. You know fucking everything. You're just mad you can't get in her pants anymore."

Enzo's face reddens as he clenches his fists.

Jesus, this is bad.

I step closer to the two of them, not wanting to position myself right in the middle but thinking I might distract them and make them realize what meatheads they're being.

I place a hand on either guy's shoulder. "Hey, this isn't going to help. We're facing some big-ass challenges. We need to stick together. Not turn on each other."

Owen pushes my hand off. "Okay, fine, Mister Perfect. Like you have no part in this shitshow. You're the one who was pushing to expand to begin with. Turned Livvy against us right from the start."

Is he being serious?

"If you remember, first of all, Owe, you and Enzo were on board with the idea. And we made her a fair offer. We weren't looking to push her out or cheat her in any way. It was her prerogative to tell us no, which she did. We never pressured her. So I don't see how that contributed to a bad relationship, nor to the imminent downfall of EastSide."

Owen jumps to his feet and gets right in my face. "Downfall? There isn't going to be any downfall here, I can promise you that. If you don't believe in what we're doing, there door's right there," he growls.

Enzo gets to his feet, looking between the two of us, like he might have to break something up, but it's not necessary. I back up. I need to get the hell out of here.

I was right. The demise of EastSide equals the demise of our relationships. With a heavy heart, I take my drink and head back to my office to get away from the toxicity of my business partners.

I look at this week's numbers. If they're just an anomaly, we'll be fine. But if this is indicative of what lies ahead, we've got a problem.

Maybe it's time to dicker with the developers. Get out while the business is still worth something. Because if we wait until the day we close our doors, I can guarantee no one's going to pay shit for this place.

48

LIVVY

WITH MY HAIR pulled up into the world's ugliest struggle bun, sporting the nasty free T-shirt my bank gave out that I normally use for dusting, I start doing something I thought I'd never have to.

I'm marking down my fancy dog and cat clothing. Putting it all on sale. The manufacturers at Cucci were kind enough to send me one more small box of goodies, probably returns from a more successful pet store somewhere, extending me the last bit of credit they can. I don't fault them for cracking down on my deadbeat ass. They're a business like I am, and they have bills to pay.

I pull the tiny sweaters and raincoats, handmade in the outer reaches of Mongolia, out of their cardboard shipping box, and gently hang them, knowing this is the last time I'll get to do this. At the bottom of the box are a few bags of Cucci's gourmet dog treats that would put any fancy restaurant—EastSide comes to mind—to shame.

There was a time when Pawsh Pets and my sky-high ambitions were all about creating a boutique where pets weren't just animals, but royalty. How far the mighty have fallen.

With a red Sharpie, I cross the retail price of the tags, and mark each at fifty percent off.

Each one of these feels like a betrayal, a glaring, mocking judgment screaming how unimportant my aspirations are to the rest of the world. It's an exercise in torture, like marking down the value of my dreams. I have to do it, though, to raise some cash if I want to keep Pawsh open for a few more weeks.

Hope the dogs and cats of the Upper East Side appreciate this, my donation to their universe.

The doorbell jingles and for a moment I think how much I'm going to miss that sound. The next second, I'm mad at myself for assuming Pawsh Pets' demise is a foregone conclusion.

But it kind of is, right?

I look up to see what lucky patron is going to be the beneficiary of my fire sale.

It's Weston. From next door.

His timing is impeccable as a train wreck.

Of course, he's all pressed and starched like any

young master of the universe, and here I am, looking like a homeless person.

No offense to homeless people.

Harry hisses, like he always does.

I'm pretty sure I haven't put on deodorant for a week, and I don't remember if I brushed my teeth this morning. I am certain I haven't washed my hair in several days.

I jump behind the counter so Weston can't get too close. It's one thing to look at me, but another to have to smell me.

"Livvy," he says, pausing at the door like I might tell him to get the hell out.

He and his buds might not be my favorite people, but I'm not that much of a bitch.

"Oh hi, Weston," I say all breezy and cool.

He gets a little closer, not quite to the front counter, but close enough I can see his slight afternoon facial scruff. If only I didn't want to run my fingers through it so badly.

"I… haven't seen you in a while."

I shrug and pretend to organize a little tray of cat crowns, the ones I just put up on Instagram. Yes, those would be crowns, worn by cats. I've never tried to put one on Harry. I value my fingers too much.

"Been busy, ya know?"

He's at the counter now and I push my stool back a little in case I stink. He doesn't seem to notice what a slob I look like.

He puts his hands on his hips and looks down, shaking his head. "I hear ya. Busy, busy, busy. Always something to do, huh?"

I want to ask him to leave, to not remind me of the mess I'm in financially... and personally. But one, I can't bring myself to do that, and two, I'm not about to let on how much I was enjoying his and the guys' company. They don't need any flattery from me, they probably get all they need on a daily basis, anyway. I don't have to wonder whether women from all over the city throw themselves at these guys—I've seen it firsthand.

"What can I do for you, Wes? You here to pick up some food for the cat that is Owen's, which he pretends is his mother's?"

He wrinkles his nose. "Owe doesn't have a cat. Does he?"

I roll my eyes. "The cat at his house. It's always there, right? It's not his mom's. It's his."

He shakes his head. "That's his cat? Huh. Never really thought about it. But anyway, I'm not here for cat food."

I know he's not here for cat food. I just don't know what else to say. A tsunami of emotion is swirling in my stomach, and it's hard to think straight.

I'm not supposed to like these guys. WTF?

"I... I just want to say... I'm sorry about how things have gone sideways."

His arms hang straight at his sides, and if I'm not

imagining it, there's a pleading in his tone. Guess they need me to help fight the developers and such.

I'm tempted to tell him I'm sorry too. Sorry that his lame-ass band-aid will do nothing to put the pieces of our partnership—and other things— back together.

But damn. His eyes, normally the epitome of confidence, logic, and even-handedness, are full of something resembling genuine regret. And that sincerity in his voice? It's making me second-guess the fortress of animosity I've built for myself over the last several days.

How do you hate something like this? I want to, but I can't.

So. Unfair.

Here's this guy who has everything a person could want, and he's just gotta be friends with me. I don't get it.

It's nice, but I don't get it.

"Another thing I wanted to bring up, Livvy, is your debt."

What?

My mouth drops open because I can't speak.

He quickly picks up the slack, knowing he's skating on thin ice. "Look, I know this is your personal business, and that you pride yourself on your independence, but Owen saw your list. He told me about your debt. And it's something I can help with."

I want to scream *get out*. I want to tell him to eat shit

and die. I want him to get hit by a cab crossing the street.

But my goddamn eyes are filling with tears, right here in front of him, at what is the most humiliating moment of my life.

So, the good-looking, blessed-in-every-way guy next door pities me? Wants to save the loser girl he and his friends were slumming with to make himself feel like a big man?

I clench my fists, digging my nails into my palms in the hope that the pain will chase away my tears, but that's stupid, I know it's stupid, and it does nothing but make my hands hurt.

Universe, how did I get here? Was I that horrible in a previous life? Because I know I haven't been that bad in this one.

A tear dribbles down my cheek and Weston reaches over the counter like he's going to wipe it away. But my phone buzzes at the same time, and I grab for it to put some more distance between the two of us.

The minute I say hello, I am sorry I accepted the call, because apparently the universe has not had enough fun fucking with me today and it's my landlord on the line.

I hold a finger up to Weston like I still have manners, and trot to the back of the shop, closing the door to my office.

"Livvy, we need to talk," he says.

"I know. I know we do," I say.

"Look, the developer has made me a very good offer. I know you can't match it, Livvy. It's impossible."

"Uh-huh," I say, holding back any more tears.

"I'm sorry, but I have to give you a deadline."

He goes on for another few minutes, but I don't really absorb what he's saying. The word *deadline* echoes around me, bouncing off walls and getting louder with every second.

I have a deadline. A deadline to leave. To get the hell out. To take a hike.

Pawsh Pets is done. I am done.

It's over.

It doesn't matter if I sell my cashmere puppy jackets for half-off. No amount of puppy jackets can help now.

Nothing can.

I return to the front of the shop where Weston is waiting for me. "That was my landlord," I mumble. "He wants me out."

His eyes widen. "What? Are you kidding?"

"The developer offered him a lot of money for the building. Money I don't have."

"Livvy, I'm trying to tell you that this doesn't have to happen," Weston says.

I look around the shop. Hopefully I can sell off some of my display pieces. It would be nice to walk away with a little money in my pocket.

The doorbell rings and Mrs. Perkins comes in, Sinbad pulling her by his leash.

"Hello," I say, forcing a little perkiness.

"Hi there, honey." She heads over to the shelf for her usual purchases.

Weston lowers his voice. "Livvy, let me help you. Let us help you."

"What? You've got to be kidding," I whisper.

Mrs. Perkins drops her things on the counter. "I'm so glad you're here, honey. If I had to go across town to that horrible Pet Outlet, it would take me all day. And besides, you have much better merchandise."

I swallow away another lump in my throat. I just cannot cry in front of a customer.

"And you, young man," she says, craning her neck to look up at Weston, "are you courting our girl Livvy here?"

Oh lord.

He suppresses a smile. "Um, well, ma'am, we are friends. You see, I'm one of the owners of the restaurant next door."

She narrows her eyes at him. "Are you the ones who got that awful review in the paper the other day?"

My gaze snaps toward Weston, who nods lightly.

"Yes. That would be us. But we're pretty sure it wasn't a legitimate review. We think the developer trying to take over the block must have paid off the writer."

Waving a hand in the air, Mrs. Perkins scoffs. "Of course, they did. Are you kidding? Now look, I have a niece, Amy, who is a blogger. You know what they are, bloggers, they write stuff for the internet?"

Weston smiles. "Yes, I've heard of bloggers before."

He sneaks a glance at me and I can see he's trying not to laugh.

"Okay. I'll tell her to do a little write up for you. I know she's been there, to your restaurant. She loves it. She even offered to take me."

Weston frowns. "Why haven't you come in?"

She takes her bag from the counter, and Sinbad starts pulling her toward the door. "I've eaten there, young man, when you had your community event for Pawsh. I think you're very nice and all, but that's not my kind of food."

I press my lips together to keep from laughing, and Weston holds the door for Mrs. Perkins.

"See you later, honey," she calls over her shoulder. We watch as Sinbad lifts his leg to pee on someone's bike tire.

Weston looks at me, Mrs. Perkins' polite insult sinking in, and I just can't help myself a moment longer.

I burst out laughing.

I laugh so hard I can't breathe, and Weston watches me in shock, probably convinced by now that I am a pyscho girl, the kind who goes from tears to laugher in a matter of seconds, the kind of girl that every smart guy knows to avoid.

But instead of bolting, he starts laughing too. The corners of his eyes crinkle, and his wide smile shows off crooked lower teeth. He actually leans onto the counter for support, laying his head on his arm, until he's done.

I am so surprised to see him crack up I almost stop laughing myself. Almost.

While I watch Weston, I go back to his comment that I don't have to leave this place. That he may be able to help me.

If he really means that, then I suppose I could make a deal with the devil. Maybe the olive branch he extended isn't as poisonous as it seems.

Because at some point, pride and forgiveness don't matter a hell of a lot.

Not when survival does.

Priorities, yo.

Do I step aside and watch everything I've built crumble like a house of cards? Or swallow my bruised ego and see what Weston means when he offers help?

That would mean teaming up with the very men who shattered my trust, but with my back against the wall as it is, the answer is as clear as it is complicated. I need all the help I can get and I'd be a fucking prideful fool for turning any away.

I could lose my business… or set my ego aside and accept help. Of course, this means my entanglement with the guys will need some… consideration.

Hell, I need all the allies I can get right now, and it seems like it's time to repair the relationships that were growing to mean more to me than I ever cared to admit.

49

ENZO

Damn if Weston didn't work his pretty-boy magic on Livvy.

I don't know what he said or did, but she's here now, in Weston's tin can of an office. Why we're crammed in here when we have other places we could go—like the restaurant downstairs—is beyond me, but while we're all side-eyeing each other, embarrassed by the litany of conflicts that've erupted over the last few days. I think we're finally committed to doing the work we need to in order to keep our businesses healthy.

Swallowing one's pride might not be easy or even pleasant, but when your back is up against the wall, like mine literally is at this moment in Weston's office, you realize it's a small sacrifice to make to save something

309

you've poured your heart and soul into for the past two-plus years.

We guys created something amazing. We have a solid business. We can't let one setback send us running like scared little bitches.

Just like it's hard to fathom that EastSide is facing some pretty big challenges, the same goes for Livvy's shop.

From the outside, her little boutique, with its cream and white striped awning and black-letter signage in the windows, looks like a place where fancy Parisian boutique meets canine and feline couture. Her velvet dog beds, feathered cat hats, and jeweled collars are the ultimate shopping experience for upscale pet owners and their little princes and princesses.

Who'd guess that the place currently has a black cloud hanging over its little head.

Just like EastSide does.

It's bullshit, plain and simple. And Weston seems to think he's found a possible solution.

I'm all ears. What other choice do we have?

Livvy's all business. "We need a countermove. Fast."

"I know we do, but even if we liquidate assets and pool our resources, we can't outspend the developer. Fuck me, I need a drink," Owen says, rubbing the bridge of his nose.

I laugh. "It's not even noon yet, bro."

He shrugs. "I call it stress management."

Hell, I wouldn't mind a drink, either. It's five o'clock somewhere.

"Guys… and gal… listen up." Weston says. "We don't have to buy the block. Which is a good thing, because we can't. So get this… the legal loophole Livvy found out about at City Hall, the one where we might be okay because our buildings are old, might actually work in our favor."

"Wait," I say, "I thought the developers found some way around that? You know, like we couldn't use it to our benefit or something."

Weston nods. "They did. But our lawyer let me know that with enough signatures from the community, we can get the city council to consider our case. We know we have neighborhood support. All we need is to get them to sign their names on a petition. We can declare the block a cultural landmark."

I'm all for turning a sinking ship around, and I'm usually the optimist of the bunch, but this sounds like a bit of a long shot. And yet, what is there to lose, except our business, our pride and joy, our hopes and dreams… and the ability to see Livvy every day?

"You're saying if we get enough signatures, we can tell the developer to go suck it?" Livvy asks.

Weston laughs but nods slowly. He knows this is not a done deal, just like the rest of us.

"What about the shitty review that douchebag 'food critic' wrote?" I ask, using air quotes around food critic.

Livvy clears her throat and tucks a strand of hair behind her ear. "I followed up with Mrs. Perkins. I just had to see whether she was blowing hot air or if her offer to help was sincere. Turns out she has her niece doing a whole story on the developer, his safety violations, his relationship to Bartlett Murray, and his likely bribing of the food writer. She's also going to talk up both our businesses. She says there's a big story here."

Holy crap. For the first time in days, my mood is improving. I might even clean out the grease traps later today.

So, while the tension among the four of us buzzes around like an annoying fly, hope covers everyone's faces too.

I decide to bombshell them with my idea.

"Guys. What do you think of this? We scramble, pulling all our contacts and resources together for this petition in the next few days. While we're doing that, I'll set up a little pop-up on the sidewalk out front, like a mini-street festival. We'll have a pet parade with prizes, and I'll have a few select dishes to serve."

They look at me for a moment, their mouths hanging open.

Yeah, I want to pat myself on the back, but I'm not douchey that way.

Livvy claps her hands together. "That's brilliant, Enz! We don't need money, we need signatures. I'll hit up my Insta following as well as my mailing list. Maybe

I can even call the teacher who brought her kids in for a field trip earlier this year. Put them to work for us."

Fuck yeah. Now we're cooking with gas.

"I can see it now: Upper East Side restaurant teams with luxury pet store to fight evil developer with pâte and puppy power," Weston says, rubbing his hands together.

Owen's been quiet, I suppose taking it all in. "What are the special dishes you're thinking of, Enzo?" he asks suspiciously.

I'm known for coming up with some crazy shit. Luckily, I have the guys to rein me in.

"Glad you asked, Owe. These are a few of my ideas, which, by the way, we can print up on a little menu card that includes the email addresses of the planning and development board. What do you think of 'bitter offer bites,' 'no deal dumplings,' 'failed deal fries,' and 'landgrabber lobster rolls?'"

"Don't forget the dog treats," Livvy warns.

"I could never forget dog treats," I say, and throw my arms around her, just because.

The room erupts in laughter and high fives and I am so fucking motivated I bolt out of the office to clean the grease traps before I get started on our pop-up menu items.

50

ENZO

Two days later, and the four of us are on fucking fire. An appeal for signatures went out to both Livvy's and our mailing lists, and I think we've already got all we need to make a very strong point to City Hall—that our businesses belong here, and whatever the hell the developer has up his sleeve, does not.

And yet, there's no room for resting on laurels. We're not taking a damn thing for granted. I don't want to sound paranoid, but if you get as close as we did to losing it all like we did, when you finally decide to strike back, you do it without mercy.

On the last night of our street festivities, as things wind down, there are still a lot of neighborhood stragglers and other folks like our lawyer hanging around who we talked into helping us finish up the leftover food and wine. It's so kick-ass to hang out in the street on a beautiful night, getting to know a lot of the folks I never see because I'm hidden away in the kitchen all the time.

Yup, we pulled out the big guns. I even brought my nonna on the last day. I think she got more signatures than any of us. No big surprise there. She's impossible to say no to.

Mrs. Perkins, who already told me it's unlikely she'll be by EastSide because she doesn't like our food, has been instrumental. Turns out you get a little pit bull like her on your side, and there's nothing that can't be accomplished. She even showed up with her naughty Sinbad in tow, stuffed into some gondolier outfit and miniature boat on wheels. The block is buzzing, signatures flowing like wine, and I could not be more proud of our amazing community.

Not to mention my friends and the lovely Livvy, who's regained the vibrant glow that attracted me to her in the first place. Not that she'd become any less than her beautiful self, but there was no denying the defeat in her eyes, which is now, thankfully, gone.

As we're talking and laughing, who should show up but Mister Moneybags Developer himself and his bought-and-paid-for minion—city councilperson Bartlett. The developer's pissed, especially when I serve him a bowl of my 'no deal dumplings,' which he didn't know were named after him until he'd devoured a couple.

Fancy that, he's mad because he inspired a dish? Actually, an entire menu?

Shit, most people would be proud. But then, most people have a sense of humor.

He makes the mistake of leaning over to say something to Weston, as if they are buds or something. I have no idea what until Weston decides to repeat it for the crowd.

He stretches to his full height and waves for everyone's attention. When the talking dies down, he really sticks it to the man. "Everybody, our friend the developer here just whispered in my ear he's going to sue our asses off. Now, is that a nice thing to say to people who just gave you free food and wine?"

A slow booing flits through the crowd as our lawyer speaks up. "I'm gonna warn you right now I've had a couple glasses of wine, so I'm not feeling my most professional, but can I just say, buddy, that you are full of *shit?*"

A roar swoops through the crowd, a level of noise I didn't realize this group of people could make.

"Go home, creep."

"Who invited that guy, anyway?"

"What a killjoy. Beat it, buddy, before we show you the door."

But my nonna seals the deal. "Young man, you should be ashamed of yourself, messing with a nice neighborhood like this. Now skedaddle home before I kick your ass all the way there."

That's my nonna.

Bartlett Murray, a man looking for the easy way out if I've ever seen one, inches away from the developer, then turns around and leaves, all elbows and ass as he picks up speed. The last I see of him is rounding a corner with a final glimpse over his shoulder to see if anyone's following him.

What a ridiculous man.

As the crowd thins out and my uncle takes my nonna back home, Livvy turns to me, her eyes shiny with tears, the static between us is too electric to ignore. I pull her to me in an emotional kiss, and Owen nods his head in the direction of his apartment, where we all set out to.

"I... I don't know how to thank you guys," Livvy says when we arrive, her voice breaking.

Owen's little cat—I mean his *mother's* cat—rubs against our legs like she's celebrating too.

Livvy bends to pick her up. "Look, I don't like to 'out' people, but Owe, when are you gonna just admit this little cutie is yours and not your mother's?" She's trying not to laugh.

"Whatever," he says, throwing his arms up in the air. He takes the cat from her just in time for Weston to swoop in.

Jesus, the man's already kicked off his shoes and socks. He's wasting no time.

Why the hell would he?

51

LIVVY

"Finally," Weston whispers in my ear.

The lights in Owen's apartment are low, so low I'm not even sure where he and Enzo are. They're close by, no doubt, watching intently.

Which is so fucking hot. I'm not an exhibitionist, at least I wasn't before these guys. Guess it's never too late to learn new tricks. Or however that saying goes.

So, in spite of the low light in the room, I can see Weston's smiling at me, and cripes if it's not like the heavens parting and God himself telling me everything's going to be fine, actually, more than fine. Pretty fucking amazing, when it comes down to it. I know nothing's a done deal, but I have a *feeling*, as Jewel would say.

"Finally what?" I ask him.

He tilts his head a little and studies me with a serious look. "You're finally in my arms. I've waited a long time for this."

I drop my head back and laugh. "You've waited a long time? How long is a long time?"

I'm not going to bother telling him how long I've waited for *him*—or Enzo or Owen. But I'm pretty sure it's my entire life.

"A day is too long to wait for you."

Oh my god. I had no idea Weston was such a corn-ball. But I keep my mouth shut. It's not every day a man like him is relishing his time with little old me, and it would be really asshole-ish to mock him for his purple prose.

I'll giggle later.

His mouth lands on mine, his lips soft but not too soft, unapologetic enough to say who's boss.

Or at least that he thinks he's boss.

I begin unbuttoning his starched button-down, the stiff fabric barely pliable under my fingers. But I get enough of it open to get my hands on his hard chest, and gently rake my nails through a sprinkling of chest hair. He's warm, actually more like hot, and when I brush his nipples, I swear his breath hitches the tiniest amount.

Have I found his kryptonite? Time will tell.

After the shit of the last couple weeks, it's almost a

guilty pleasure to be in his arms like this, like an indulgence I don't deserve.

Fuck that.

"I like you, Livvy," he says.

He hooks an arm around my waist and sweeps me to the arm of the sofa, which he props me against, and begins to open my jeans. I watch his long fingers hard at work, eager to touch my bare flesh.

"I like you too, Weston," I sigh.

I want him to touch me. Everywhere. I pull my blouse off over my head and reach behind myself for my bra clasp. I'm not waiting for him to take care of business. I'm not in a patient mood.

After he slides my jeans and panties down to the floor, he takes a step back and looks me up and down, like a combination hungry wolf and ardent admirer.

I'm not complaining.

His hands palm my breasts, lifting them to his mouth for kisses, kneading them, and pulling my nipples until I gasp.

"You like that," he murmurs.

I run my hands up his muscular arms, over his shoulders, and down his back. He's beautiful, solid, and strong, his touch confident and firm. If you told me a couple days ago I'd be here with Weston, with Enzo and Owen in the background, watching, I would have laughed in your face.

And gone home to eat a pint of Ben and Jerry's.

Weston's hands roam my body but it's the space

between my legs that's responding the deepest, no surprise. But he hasn't touched me there. Yet.

With my ass half-propped on the sofa arm, Weston kneels before me, spreading my legs as wide as they will go, and runs two fingers between my swollen pussy lips. Soaked, he pushes them into my mouth, my eyes falling closed as I savor my excitement, swirling my tongue and wanting more.

The tension in my sex is coiled tightly, like a rubber band about to break, and when Weston swipes his tongue from my ass to my clit in a long sweep, a shudder hits me so hard I have to grab the sofa back for balance.

"Baby," he says, and our eyes meet. "Watch me. I don't want you to miss it. Keep your eyes open. If you can." With a wicked smile, he returns to lapping me, circling my clit, and plunging inside my opening.

The frustration—and other emotions—of last week feel like they are being exorcised, driven away by lust, and I don't think there is any better medicine in the world. The pleasure of releasing my anxiety is heady and luxurious and I wish I could feel like this every day.

Weston's mouth returns to mine, his now-naked erection pressing my inner thigh. He nips my lower lip and, surprised, I yelp. His mouth remains on mine while the head of his cock slides through my wet pussy, up and down, teasing my clit.

And he still does not enter me.

Jesus, does he need a fucking engraved invitation?

"Wes," I mumble.

"Yeah, darling?"

"I think you should fuck me now."

He pulls his head back with a smirk. "Oh, okay. Baby wants some dick. Well, tell me how you like… this."

He drives inside me, filling me with the heaviness of his cock and I'm pretty sure I moan loudly, but I'm not entirely positive.

He eases out and then slams back into me, each stroke a masterpiece, building to a crescendo where he slams again and again, and I hold on for dear life by gripping his arms and wrapping my legs around his ass.

"Don't… stop…" I beg, my voice vibrating with his hard fucking.

He's reached the point inside me from where there's no return. Lost in our rutting, I spin out of control in a mind-altering explosion, my moans filling the air. Like magic, his own orgasm follows mine by seconds and we move together until we're too exhausted to continue.

52

LIVVY

I HEAD to the shop the next morning, remembering the day not that long ago where I followed Owen and his cute ass all the way to work, ducking behind bushes to make sure he didn't see me.

I have to hustle because Jewel won't be in to open the store for me. Nor will she be in tomorrow. Or the next day. She called at six a.m. to let me know she was at the airport waiting for a flight to Spain, a starting point for a backpacking trip through Europe that she wasn't sure she'd ever be returning from.

Turns out that she and her boyfriend were up most of the night making future plans. They decided to kick off their lives together by packing and heading straight to the airport to catch the first flight they could get out of the country.

Well, damn.

I couldn't be mad. In fact, I was thrilled for her. I'd miss her, yes. She added a lot of light to my life the last couple years with her zany ways.

Goodbye, Jewel.

I open up Pawsh and, after feeding Harry, fiddle with my merchandise, obsessed as always with making sure my merchandise is lovingly displayed for my customers' fur babies. If you're going to charge five-hundred dollars for a cashmere dog bed, it should darn well be displayed like the freaking Hope diamond.

This simultaneously calms me, as it always has, and lets my mind wander to the night before, when the guys ravished me til the wee hours of the morning. I finally left them, exhausted and sleeping in Owen's apartment, to head home to grab some solo sleep before a long day at the shop.

On one hand, my heart is doing cartwheels because the guys and I have defeated our own personal Goliath, but something in me is guarding that optimism.

Is that because I don't think I deserve this? Or that I'm afraid, deep down, that someone, at any moment, will pull the rug out from under me with a *Psyche! You thought you really made it, didn't you?*

God, why can't I just enjoy a nice moment without overthinking it?

When I'm satisfied the shop looks about as zen-like

as it can, I peel open a protein bar and start to munch on it, straightening out pet treats with my free hand. Behind me, the bells rings, and who comes in but Owen, Weston, and Enzo. They are bearing a funny little cactus, which Owen thrusts at me.

The plant is ridiculously small, dwarfed by Owen's hand, and when he passes to me, it doesn't look like it could possibly be real. What is real though is the sincere look on the guys' faces. Their sentiment is so pure that the last remnants of my protective shell seem like they might finally be taking their leave.

Is that even possible?

I get it. I know what the guys are saying. A new plant for a new beginning.

"Thank you," I say, humbled by the baby succulent. "I just love it."

Enzo is first to speak. "Livvy. We've got some cool ideas to run past you."

I look from one of the guys to the next. "You haven't let me down yet. Let's hear it."

Enzo is practically vibrating. "I'm going to create a pet menu. Food for dogs whose owners are dining with us."

Damn him. Why didn't I think of that?

"Okay, that rocks but you can't have animals in the restaurant."

Owen taps the side of his head like he's some sort of genius. "You are correct, pretty girl. However, given the disgrace of our council member Bartlett, he's looking for a way to redeem himself. He can help us get a special variance."

"Are you kidding?" I ask, blown away.

"And that's not all," he adds. "Imagine this… 'Pawtio dining,' an EastSide exclusive. Sunday doggy brunch. Pet adoption weekends. The dog food branding will be a collaboration between the restaurant and Pawsh. We'll each provide the other credibility and goodwill. You can carry the dog food here in Pawsh too. It's almost a merging of our businesses. We'll provide a one-of-a-kind, pet friendly dining experience."

For a moment, I see what my life with these guys could be like—and endless parade of fun and collaboration, trying new ideas, and never letting things get stale.

As Enzo continues, with Weston adding the financial angle, and Owen offering his PR thoughts, I'm stuck by a lightning bolt of exhilaration. Enzo's crazy quilt of a business proposition makes perfect sense, hitting me like a dream that promises to take both our businesses to the next level.

I shake my head. "I love it. When do we start?"

The guys laugh. "I need some time to develop dog food. That is not something they teach at the culinary academy."

Oh. Right. Hadn't thought of that. "I'm sure I can put you in touch with some of my distributors. They'll probably be very interested in what you're doing."

"Holy shit," Enzo says, high-fiving his friends.

"But you know, we do have some details to iron out," I say.

The guys nod like it's a foregone conclusion, and that they'll worry about it another day.

Not so fast.

"I want to lay down my terms. They're important to me."

They straighten up when they realize how serious I am.

"Of course, baby. Tell us what you're thinking," Owen says, grabbing me and planting a juicy kiss on my cheek.

"Okay. First, my brand needs to be as visible as yours. I want a say in what goes into the dog food. And any employees I have will be part of this too."

The guys nod and I realize they are not just agreeing with me but they also respect me. They're not just paying me lip service, telling me what I want to hear so they can get back to work, but they really want my input. They plan to incorporate my interests, and that makes me feel validated.

"There's one other thing, Livvy," Weston says.

"What's that?"

"I want you to let me help with your debt. I have the money and I can't think of a better place to invest it," he says.

A lump starts to build in my throat but this is not the time to cry, so I run to the back of the shop and retrieve the cheap bottle of champagne Jewel left behind. We each take a paper cup of it. It's so nasty we can't tolerate more than a ceremonial sip.

"To new beginnings," I say, looking at each of their faces.

There's Enzo, wearing his emotions on his sleeve, Owen with his irresistible charm, and Weston with his uncanny ability to make sense out of chaos. For the first time in a long time, I'm excited about what comes next. And I'm not just talking about my business but my relationship with these three beautiful men. There's so much that's yet to be determined, but the one thing I'm sure of is how much I care for these guys. More than I ever thought possible.

I'm on the cusp of something big. I know it. Where it will lead, well, that remains to be seen. But what is certain is that I'm no longer a bystander in life. I'm an active participant who can make shit happen.

And no matter what does happen, all will be well with my three restauranteurs by my side.

EPILOGUE
LIVVY

Maybe there's something to all that law of attraction mumbo jumbo Jewel introduced me to. I'm actually begin-

ning to think it's not so far-fetched after all. I shot her an update recently to let her know things in both Pawsh-land and Livvy-land are looking up. Not fairy-tale perfect, not by any stretch of the imagination, but they're definitely looking up, which is all I can hope for. Her ecstatic response? She was thrilled and told me to keep meditating for even brighter days. "The universe is listening!" she wrote.

I don't have the heart to tell her I never actually meditated. Instead, I just pasted the instructions she gave me on the wall by my desk, and looked at them from time to time.

But love, now that's something I have spent a lot of time lately thinking about, even if it's not meditating in the conventional sense, which I suck at anyway. The whirlwind of emotions swirling around me thanks to the three gorgeous men next door is enough to put anyone in a trance.

Either way, I am one satisfied customer.

Jewel also let me know she and her boyfriend were about to start working on some big fishing boat in the Mediterranean, and that I might not hear from them again until they reached Northern Africa.

Lucky for her, she likes to eat fish.

From time to time, I still look over at the law of attraction stuff hanging by my desk and have to wonder, was it really believing in and appealing to it that got me where I am today? Did it work its magic on little old me? Who knows. Part of me wants to believe in it because if I ever need anything else for future challenges, I can tap into it again. But I'm also a firm believer in creating your own fate—that the universe is mostly indifferent and you have to make your own luck. Sometimes that works and sometimes it doesn't. The way everything worked out for me, could just as easily have gone in the opposite direction.

But it didn't, so I'm not dwelling on it.

Thanks to Amy, Mrs. Perkins' blogger niece, and her write-ups, things have livened up at Pawsh again and the cash register is singing sweet melodies. I'm not saying I'm going to get rich from selling pet stuff, but I'm confidently back in business, so to speak, paying my bills on time without sweating over it.

As he'd offered before, Weston, ever the knight, generously wanted to use his own money to bail me out of my debt. He really believes in me and Pawsh. I ended up accepting his offer as a loan—or an investment as he puts it. I insisted on making monthly payments to him. He thinks it's silly, but he understands I need to stand on my own two feet as a testament to my independence.

I actually had the chance to meet up with the blogger, who gave me some tips to keep the buzz around Pawsh alive, like having weekly pet adoption events with the local animal shelter. Brilliant idea. People from all over the city are coming here now if only to see the adorable kittens and puppies. And every time someone adopts a pet, which they often do, they get a gift certificate to Pawsh as a cherry on top. It keeps them coming back, for sure.

Then, after taking in a new fur baby, people pop in next door for a drink and a nibble to celebrate.

See, Enzo has tweaked the menu there.

The guys still serve all kinds of weird and crazy-expen-

sive carnivore delights, but they added a lighter menu so everyone—not just those who are loaded—can enjoy their restaurant.

I love that. Something for everyone.

For all she's done for us, not least of which was introducing us to her niece, Mrs. Perkins now gets free dog food for life. She'd also get free human food from EastSide, but has made it clear she has no interest in what they are serving. Imagine, turning down some of the best food in the city. But hey, if you don't like it, you don't like it.

Speaking of the best food in the city, the blogger exposed a whole big story about how the food critic who tried to tank EastSide was on the take and was full of shit. He wrote a tearful retraction, recommended EastSide with the highest possible praise, and resigned. He left the city with his tail between his legs just as he should, and EastSide is soaring again.

In fact, they're so busy, we hardly get to see each other. But when we do, watch out. We always make up for lost time.

The restaurant critic was not the only person to go down in disgrace. Turns out Bartlett Murray did as well, although his downfall took a little longer. He spent the rest of his term bending over backwards doing nice things for EastSide and Pawsh since he played such a big role in trying to get rid of us. But when re-election time rolled around, it turned out no amount of goodwill could save his sorry ass. Our district voted him out with a bang.

Arthur came by last week to check out the animals on pet

adoption day. When he got there too late—all the kitties were gone—I asked him if he wanted to take Harry home for a couple days to see how it worked out. I brought him into the store and he and the cat stared each other down for a while. Then, miracle of miracles, Harry walked over to Arthur and rubbed on him.

That cat doesn't even rub on me.

I couldn't freaking believe it, but I think those two had some sort of meeting of the minds. I would have figured two divas would repel each other like oil and water, but it's more like they get each other. God knows they deserve each other.

Yikes. I'm sounding like Jewel.

So now, these two are living in domestic bliss, unbelievable as that sounds. I do watch Harry when Arthur's out of town though, so it's not like my mascot is gone completely. And he still has the nerve to hiss at me, even though I got him the home of his dreams. Seriously, Harry treats him like a king.

Do I miss having him in the shop every day? A little. But it's nice not to have to keep an eye on him, waiting for him to turn one of my customer's pets into a meal.

Thanks to the press we got, which started with the blogger's exposé shedding light on the safety violations of the developer trying to take the block, they are now on probation here in New York, finally paying fines for their mess-ups. I'm not sure how they slipped through the cracks for so long, but I did hear some people in City Hall got fired over it. It's not been hard to figure out that Bartlett wasn't the only person the developer was paying off.

Those creeps were spending a lot of money to get rid of us. And look at them now.

When the Kritters learned I not only had a new man in my life, but actually three, they finally stopped trying to fix me up with their friends. Sure, they were aghast at our arrangement initially, but when Krista got a load of the guys, she changed her tune. Now, she finds all the excuses she can to come into the city with her creep husband and dine at EastSide. I can't blame her. I like being around them, too.

As for BOB, it turned out his battery hadn't just run out, his entire mechanism had died from old age. Guess adult toys have a limited shelf life. That's how they get us to buy new ones, right? A person might assume I no longer need a vibrator or any other kind of toy, now that I've got the guys. That's what I initially thought, too. But it turns out they are lots of fun to use with a partner.

Or partners.

Mrs. Johnson and her chubby beagle lost weight together. They look great, and take long walks in Central Park when the weather's nice. She couldn't be happier knowing her boy will be with her a good long time, and now wants to make sure she's around for him, too. Unfortunately, she's not too happy about Pawsh's recent successes. She says the blogger ruined everything, and now the shop is always jammed, too crowded for her leisurely visits. She preferred the place when it was a quiet little Upper East Side shop. I know she's happy for me though, she just misses the old days when we could hang out and gossip.

I told her fame has its downsides. She didn't think that was funny.

What is it about pets, sharing our homes, and taking care of innocent little creatures who comfort us as much as we comfort them?

Okay, Harry wasn't that innocent. But still.

And what is it about the magic of good food, sharing it with friends, creating new rituals, and expanding our palettes?

What's that old saying?

'Happiness shared is happiness doubled."

Or something like that.

With life back on track, I keep pinching myself, waiting for something to go awry. Because it will. It always does. Things are never perfect.

And next time things start going sideways, I won't be devastated. Problems will be more like a blip on the screen. Because when the three gorgeous men next door have your back, you know you can stand up to most anything trying to knock you down.

They know I've got their backs too.

Who would have thought three foodie masters of the universe would have a soft spot for the quirky girl next door?

Not me.

But no one would have thought this girl next door could ever have feelings in return for the hot bistro boys.

I know I didn't.

If you enjoyed Livvy's story, check out the next sizzling story from Mika Lane:
From Puck to F*ck,
a perfect combination of fun and sizzle about a sports hater and the hockey player she falls for.

Dear Reader:

I'm USA TODAY bestselling romance author Mika Lane, and am OBSESSED with bringing you sassy, steamy stories with imperfect heroines and the bad-a*s dudes they bring to their knees. I'll always bring you my signature humor and heat, topped off with a modern-day happily ever after.

My first book ever was *The Day I Ate the Milkyway*, a true fourth-grade masterpiece illustrated with crayons and bound with construction paper and glue. Nowadays, steamy romance gives purpose to my days and nights as I create worlds and characters that tickle the imagination. I live in magical Northern California with my own handsome alpha dude, sometimes known as Mr. Mika Lane, and two devilish cats named Chuck and Murray.

A dual citizen of the United States and Ireland, I have on more than one occasion spent my last dollar on a plane ticket somewhere, and am always planning my next escape. I often try new recipes on unsuspecting friends, search out hiding places to read undisturbed, and sadly kill every houseplant I bring home.

I LOVE to hear from readers when I'm not dreaming up naughty tales to share. Visit my online shop https://mikalaneshop.com/ and say hello https://mikalaneshop.com/pages/meet-mika.

xoxo, Mika